FATE

FATE

EDENTU OROSO

Contents

To my lovelies: Princess, Tarebi, Angel, Preye,

Stephanie!

ACKNOWLEDGEMENTS

I am deeply grateful to my family for standing by me through thick and thin, offering unwavering love and support that has shaped my journey as a writer.

To my fans around the world, your tireless encouragement has been a constant source of inspiration; your belief in my work keeps me going.

I extend my heartfelt thanks to Abigail Wild, Founder/Creative Director of Wild Ink Publishing, USA, for her faith in this book project. Your exceptional design for the cover and the professionalism you brought to bear in making this dream a reality are truly appreciated.

Author's Note

In writing *FATE*, I aimed to create a collection that offers a deeper understanding of man's true nature and the world we inhabit. With the exception of "Cockroach-X," which employs fictional elements and a satirical lens, and "The Stolen Knoodle Recipe,' which is purely imaginative, every narrative in this collection is grounded in true life experiences—some from individuals living and others from those who have passed. Also, some of these stories emerged from personal revelations or interactions with people who have shared their profound experiences with me, as well as from tales recounted by those who knew them.

At its core, *FATE* provides a glimpse into the paranormal and metaphysical realms. It delves into the ridiculous and the sublime of the

African cosmology, exploring the supernatural while transcending the boundaries of our perceptions. This collection illuminates as well pristine beginnings and unthinkable possibilities, expanding the frontiers of our imaginations with what is plausible and what exists beyond the limits of our senses.

Through the blend of authentic narratives and spiritual exploration, *FATE* invites readers to confront the complexities of life, death, and the unseen forces that shape our journeys. It is my hope that these stories foster a deeper appreciation for the diversity of human experience and the shared quest for meaning that transcends cultural boundaries.

Ultimately, *FATE* weaves together threads of reality, spirituality, and imagination. It aims to provide not just stories, but a lens through which we can better understand ourselves and the myriad forces that connect us all in this intricate tapestry of life. Thank you for joining me on this journey.

GODS and GODDESSES

The Hunter

A HARSH GRINDING NOISE cut through the silence, like iron grating against iron—Perekebena Ebiotu's kola nut-stained teeth pressed together. His broad shoulders quaked, the tremor rippling through his muscular frame as the messenger's words sank in.

Teina, his younger cousin, had fallen. The dreaded Maenarr had claimed another life, another victim ensnared by the spirit's malevolent power deep within Okoloba forest. Perekebena's chest rose and fell with each breath, his heart pounding a steady, ominous rhythm. There was no more room for hesitation; the time had come to face the darkness that lurked in the woods.

His eyes, dark and intense, flared with an inner fire that refused to be quenched. Without another word, he turned on his heel, storming into the depths of his block house. The walls seemed to tremble with the force of his passage, a testament to the storm that raged within him.

When he reappeared, a transformation had taken place. A torn khaki overall clung to his frame, the fabric stretched tight over sinewy muscles. A red bandana crowned his head, tied with a deliberate knot. An animal skin bag hung from his shoulder, and a double-barreled gun rested in the crook of his arm. His movements were fluid, deliberate, each step echoing with a predator's certainty.

He walked past the gathering crowd, their hushed whispers and tear-streaked faces met with a hardened gaze. A low tune, ominous and steady, hummed from deep within his chest, the rhythm of a warrior preparing for battle.

As he reached the edge of the forest, a few brave souls tried to follow, their hands reaching out in a futile attempt to hold him back.

"No one follows me," he said, the command leaving no room for argument. His voice cut through the air, freezing them in place. They watched as he disappeared into the trees, knowing this was a journey he would undertake alone.

Moments later, Perekebena Ebiotu pressed his back against the rough bark of a towering raffia tree, his breath shallow as he tightened his grip on the gun. The dense, humid air of the rainforest clung to him, amplifying the slightest sound. A rapid, slithering movement in the nearby thicket seized his attention. He scanned the area, his eyes narrowing at the faint impressions left in the damp earth—trampled grass and broken twigs tracing an eastward path through the undergrowth.

His heart pounded as the shape ahead shifted again, its form elusive, blending with the forest's shadows. Instinct honed by years of hunting told him it was close—too close. Ebiotu's finger hovered over the trigger, the weight of the moment thick in the air.

Then, through the tangled mess of ferns and towering trees, his gaze locked onto a small clearing—a circle of undisturbed ground, framed by the towering silhouettes of raffia palms. The space was eerily still, a stark contrast to the chaotic greenery around it. The creature had paused there, waiting, perhaps sensing his presence. A bead of sweat trickled down Ebiotu's brow as the tension in the forest reached a breaking point.

Ebiotu's voice cut through the thick silence of the forest, his words a sharp whisper laced with venom. "Come out now, you cursed beast. No tricks will save you this time." His finger tensed on the trigger, eyes narrowing as he scanned the tangled web of trees before him.

The forest seemed to conspire against him, its tall trees and dense underbrush swallowing the rising sun's light. Only a single, thin beam pierced through the canopy, casting a narrow strip of daylight onto the forest floor. Ebiotu stood in the darkness beneath a raffia palm, feeling the weight of the atmosphere pressing down on him. The air was heavy, still. Not a leaf rustled, not a branch stirred. He gritted his teeth, forcing his breathing to slow, trying to steady his nerves.

His rain boots made an unsettling, hollow pop as he shifted his weight, the sound amplified in the unnatural silence. His feet sank deeper into the mire, the squelching of mud and decaying leaves threatening to engulf him. The smell was overwhelming—a foul blend of rot, wet earth, and crude oil that churned his stomach. Ebiotu fought back the urge to retch, the stench clinging to him like the muck that rose up his legs.

"Damn it," he cursed inwardly, casting a quick glance at the ground beneath him. The thought of being trapped in this forsaken mire made his pulse quicken. With a sharp tug, he pulled the gun strap across his shoulder, freeing his right hand. He reached out to a low-hanging branch, gripping it with white-knuckled desperation. The branch bowed under his weight before snapping back, propelling him out of the mire and onto firmer ground.

Ebiotu moved forward, his steps cautious but determined. His eyes never left the shifting shadows ahead, where the creature lurked just out of sight. The forest seemed to hold its breath as he advanced, each step a test of his resolve. The oppressive quiet was broken only by the sound of his own breath, ragged and strained. The smell, that god awful smell, lingered in his nostrils, threatening to unravel his focus. He pulled a lobe of kola nut from his hunting bag and bit into it, hoping the bitterness would settle his stomach.

But it wasn't just the stench that gnawed at him. It was the uncertainty—the not knowing whether he was the hunter or the hunted. Fear slithered up his spine, coiling around his resolve, but he shook it off. His eyes were sharp, trained for the slightest movement. Yet, it was the stillness that unnerved him most—the sense that something was out there, watching, waiting.

Ebiotu pressed on, his senses heightened, every nerve on edge. The creature could be anywhere—in the trees above, slithering through the underbrush, or perhaps, right behind him. The forest closed in around him, a living, breathing entity that seemed to whisper secrets in the windless air. He felt the weight of those whispers, their malevolent intent curling in his gut.

As he edged closer to where he last saw the creature, the forest grew darker, the light from the sun all but extinguished. Ebiotu swallowed hard, forcing his fear down, deep into the pit of his stomach. He had no choice now but to confront whatever awaited him in the shadows.

The glaring absence of birds singing warnings or ushering good tidings of the day's offerings on tree tops – a normal part of his daily hunting sprees – troubled him. Why is the forest so silent? Why are the messengers of the gods, the chirpy birds, not speaking this morning?

Ebiotu cringed at the thought that he had become the prey rather than the hunter; held hostage by the inexplicable nature of the shape-shifter under the canopy of trees in the near blanket darkness of early morning. How many times had he as a hunter felt so cagey? It invoked his instinct for survival.

Ebiotu's breath caught as the memory surged back—a leopard's charge, four years ago, in the forest across the river. He had barely escaped with his life, his spine almost snapping under the weight of his terror. The scene had shrunk his world to a pinhole, a narrow glimpse into death's realm. The leopard's fierce eyes and the earth-shaking roar as he fired his last shot haunted him still. He could feel the heat of the animal's breath, the vibration of its crash into the brush just inches from his body, the cold sweat on his skin as he staggered back, his final shot a desperate plea for survival.

Fear had seeped into his bones that day, and now, it returned with a vengeance. His heart hammered, adrenaline surging as he gripped his gun, his last shield against the inevitable. He scanned the clearing again, his eyes narrowing.

There—movement.

Something emerged from the shadows, a tall, animal-like figure, shrouded in a swirling mist, not thirty meters away. It moved with a deadly grace, claiming the space between the waterlogged ground and the dense trees. Ebiotu's finger tightened on the trigger, every muscle in his body coiled, ready to fight or flee.

Ebiotu steadied his aim, his breath shallow as he calculated the perfect shot. He could end it all now, put a bullet through the heart of this wretched creature, and be done with it. But the weight of the moment pressed against his chest, whispering doubts. *Would I survive the retaliation?* The thought gnawed at him, but the fire in his belly surged stronger. Better to go down fighting, defending his life, than to cower in the shadows.

His finger curled around the trigger, ready to unleash the kill shot, when a voice cut through the silence of the clearing, snapping him back to the present.

"Don't shoot." The words were calm, unnervingly so. "It isn't necessary. You can't kill what's already dead."

A cold wave swept over Ebiotu, freezing his blood in its path. For a moment, his heart stumbled, but then, fueled by raw defiance, he spat back, "Who dares stop a lion from claiming his prey?" His voice, though tinged with fear, held a flicker of resolve. "Show yourself, you foolish beast or whatever you are."

Laughter, low and mocking, echoed from the shadows. "Listen to yourself," the figure taunted, its tone dripping with contempt. "A perfect example of man's arrogance. Always boasting about things he barely understands."

Ebiotu's forefinger slackened on the gun's trigger, stunned by those words. "I'm a legend in this forest. I fear no animal or man," he boasted, feigning some level of confidence.

A harsh, mocking laugh echoed from the darkness. "Typical of a fool. Men all wear the same robes of foolishness. Arrogant, yet blind as bats in the sun. Don't waste my time with these empty words, hunter."

Ebiotu's mind raced, thoughts crashing into one another like waves in a storm. *He knows what I do? Damn!*

"They all think they're untouchable. Fools! We see through you all, mortals."

The words cut deep, eating away at Ebiotu's resolve like acid on skin. Fear gnawed at the edges of his courage, but he clenched his jaw. He wouldn't flee.

A sudden rustle of leaves and a gust of wind snapped his attention back to the clearing. Where the whirlwind had raged moments before, a skeleton now stood, its empty eyes locked onto Ebiotu. The red glint in its sockets mirrored the look of a dying animal caught in the sights of his smoking gun.

Ebiotu's instinct screamed at him to run, but his feet remained rooted. He had hunted for fifteen years, but nothing had prepared him for this—a confrontation with a spirit wearing the bones of the dead. The forest, usually a cacophony of natural life, now felt like a prison. The trees closed in, their branches reaching out like skeletal hands, the pine grass tangled around his boots, and the birds' songs warped into eerie, mocking jeers. The air thickened with the weight of a thousand unseen eyes.

"There's no need to panic," the skeleton's voice hissed through the wind, as casual as if they were discussing the weather. "Make a wish, hunter. I'm obliged to grant it."

"A wish?" Ebiotu's voice cracked, the only sign of his trembling resolve. He blinked, forcing his focus on the ghastly figure before him.

"Yes, a wish."

The word echoed in his mind, taunting him. *What do I ask for? What could possibly help me now?* "I desire spiritual sight," he finally breathed out.

"Granted," the skeleton boomed, its voice reverberating through the trees.

Ebiotu tightened his grip on his gun, the cold metal his only comfort. "Who—who are you?" he demanded, trying to mask his fear with bravado.

"That's irrelevant, my friend," the skeleton replied, dismissing the question with a wave of its bony hand. "What matters is why I am what I am."

"Why?" Ebiotu's voice steadied, emboldened by the strange exchange. He forced himself to meet the creature's gaze, daring it to reveal more.

"My tongue," the skeleton said, a hint of regret lacing its words.

"Your tongue? What does that mean?" Ebiotu asked, confusion momentarily overshadowing his fear.

"My tongue led to my death."

"Were you human once?" Ebiotu asked, the pieces of this twisted puzzle starting to fall into place.

"Isn't it obvious?" the shape-shifter scoffed. "Maybe I should tell you a story you'd like to hear."

The skeleton spread its arms wide, and the forest responded. The leaves swayed to a rhythm, and melodies from another realm filled the air. Ebiotu stood transfixed, the music lulling his mind into a state of numb awe. He couldn't move, couldn't speak, as the skeleton began a haunting, lyrical chant, its bony form swaying like a madman lost in a twisted dance:

I will speak of great beginnings,

the dawn entwined with destiny's thread.

Stars sparkled across the void, but never enough

to bathe the realms in light's full embrace.

Lives took flight beyond the threshold,

from the sweltering furnace of time's womb.

The forge birthed the ether's condensation,

and Providence spun its wheels.

Planes unfurled in concentric rings,

ether upon ether, consciousness swirled with dust.

Soul's alchemy of knowledge twirled through space,

until we became human, souls in disguise,

tasked with basking in the glory of action;

infinitesimal steps in a gigantic pod,

seeking to redefine a pristine promise.

This is not an ode,

nor a testament of codes,

no trumpeting harps for the journeying soul.

Your stage is a shard of glimpsed promises,

a regatta for the next vital ascent.

From realms far beyond, they came,

to thresh here in the now, over bouquets of experiences.

But those of your kind who put spanners in the wheels—

you have yet to grasp the inchoate fire of being,

burnishing away the form's cloaks,

lighting paths to the One brilliance.

Here you stand, a conquering matador,

but are you the victor or the vanquished?

Is this your true success?

Or merely a life well spent, on a leash?

You're but a slave to the flesh's demands,

but I have come as your liberating force,

a complex puzzle you must unravel,

a trickling from the void,

the same crystal you chased from afar.

When the rites are done,

will you remember the journey's nature?

The descent and ascent,

on the crest of the ether's sea as an angel?

How you squander talents,

chasing creation's illusions.

You're adrift in this vast sea,

a rudderless sail on an unsteady keel.

Time is a commodity you lack.

Find your bearings,

like a moth drawn to a flame,

to the sky you were always told of.

The source you seek is within.

Is there truth in the gun

you wield with practiced hands?

A bitter reminder of your fall

from gilded realms.

Can the broken halo be mended?

Only love can.

Fierce warrior,

I feel your heart's pulse.

You carry the weight of fear,

a shroud on your shoulders.

You're the bowstring of God,

upon which experiences are struck.

All you ever wanted was to be unleashed,

a tiny spark of the whole.

You could be a piece of heaven,

if only you seek the beauty within.

The skeleton's singsong trailed off, leaving Perekebena Ebiotu gasping in relief. He couldn't shake the certainty that something otherworldly had just unfolded—a flash of light in the unseen.

"Go now," the skeleton's voice rasped, its tone a haunting echo. "Become whatever you choose. But remember, my downfall came from my own tongue. Return here when you need me."

Like a fleeting wind, the apparition vanished, yet its words clung to Ebiotu's mind, reverberating through the dense forest like the clash of cymbals.

His journey back to Okoloba village was a fractured memory, a series of disjointed images: the moment he collapsed after the skeleton disappeared, the rough hands that lifted his limp, muddy body from the forest floor, and the sudden awakening among familiar faces, his clothes mysteriously changed. But the clarity of his thoughts couldn't dispel the looming sense of dread.

When Ebiotu recounted his encounter to the villagers, his voice brimmed with theatrical zeal. He painted vivid pictures, his words desperate to convince, but he saw the doubt etched in their eyes. The more he embellished, the deeper their disbelief seemed to root.

"If you doubt me, come," Ebiotu challenged. "I'll take you to the spot. The skeleton promised he'd be there."

The villagers hesitated, then a few young men agreed to follow. They set off, crossing the shallow stream that circled the village, then trudging through the thick forest. Birds of every hue serenaded them, a chorus that Ebiotu took as a sign.

"He'll be there," he boasted.

A skeptical villager sneered. "Trusting a skeleton? You must be mad."

"Not if you'd seen what I did," Ebiotu shot back, conviction tightening his voice.

Their trek through the muck and decaying leaves led them to a clearing. They hid behind raffia palms, hearts pounding, waiting.

Minutes stretched into hours. The tension became unbearable.

"How much longer do we wait?" one of the young men asked, frustration sharpening his tone. "We've been duped."

Another agreed, "We should head back. Ebiotu has made fools of us."

But the oldest among them, a weathered man with the patience of a hunter, held up a hand. "Give him the benefit of the doubt. Truth may yet reveal itself."

But truth remained elusive. After two more agonizing hours, they dragged a defeated Ebiotu back to the village, their anger erupting in a storm of curses.

They denounced him as a liar before the council, for in their world, a man's word was sacred.

When the stones started to fly, Ebiotu remembered too late the skeleton's warning: "My tongue was responsible for my downfall."

Pain exploded through him, each rock a reminder of his folly. The cries of his loved ones filled the air as darkness closed in.

In his final moments, a figure loomed in his fading vision—the skeleton, now smiling.

"What treachery is this?" Ebiotu's soul raged. "You promised you'd be there when I returned, but you abandoned me!"

The apparition's laughter echoed in the void. "How fickle humans are. Always showing off, never cautious."

"What do you mean?"

"I kept my promise."

"How can you say that? I'm dying because of you!"

The skeleton, now a fully realized being, grinned. "Death? A mere illusion. You're only transitioning, if I allow it."

Confusion clouded Ebiotu's thoughts. He tried to rise, but felt weightless, drifting instead. "If you allow it? Who are you? God?"

The being chuckled. "A concept, nothing more. You're a god too."

"Then why am I dying?"

"You're not dying. You're changing. You carry a message back to the living."

"A message?"

"You are the message," the being said with finality, and then vanished.

Ebiotu jolted awake to the wails of his family, scattering the villagers in fear. The skeleton's song echoed in his mind, its meaning sinking in:

So we became human in the guise of soul,
with the task of basking in the glory of action;
infinitesimal steps in a gigantic pod,
seeking to redefine the purpose of a pristine promise.

This is not an ode,

a testament of codes,

no trumped harps, for the journeying soul.

Your stage is a shard of glimpsed promises,

and a regatta for the next vital ascent.

Those who came from the realms far beyond,

to thresh here in the now over bouquets of experiences

and those of your kind who put spanners in the wheels

you have yet to come to terms with the inchoate fire of being

burnishing away the form's cloaks, lighting paths to the One brilliance.

Is this the message? Ebiotu pondered, wrestling to make sense of the events that had just unfolded. Or was the being alluding to another part of the refrain?

Time is a commodity you lack.

Find your bearings,

like a moth drawn to a flame,

to the sky you were always told of.

The source you seek is within.

Is there truth in the gun

you wield with practiced hands?

A bitter reminder of your fall

from gilded realms.

Can the broken halo be mended?

Only love can.

TOUCHED BY A PRIESTESS!

OGIDIGBO LINGERED AT THE shallow end of the shimmering lake, her gaze locked on Igho's rhythmic dance and chant at the headland. Her lips curved into a knowing grin, for she understood well that nothing spurred action more than the fervor of a devoted servant.

"Priestess! You summoned me," Ogidigbo's voice rippled through the stillness, her scaly caudal fin slicing the lake's placid surface, sending shivers through the moonlit waters. The crescent moon's yellow beams caught her form, casting an ethereal glow on her emerald eyes, which now flickered with an inner flame. A glittering crown of sapphires rested upon her small head, the sunburned hair beneath it shimmering like molten gold.

Igho, in the jaded light of the moon, beheld a vision that sent tremors of awe through her. Ogidigbo's silhouette, adorned with fleecy curls and the glint of a golden scepter in her hand, embodied the primal majesty of a goddess from ancient times. The air thickened with reverence as Ogidigbo's nails, long and meticulously groomed, traced the silken shawls draped over her slender figure, revealing the contours of her body. Her heaving chest, where two mounds of flesh rose like succulent mangoes, gleamed with an almost forbidden allure.

Igho, now fully entranced, ceased her chant. Her smile, tinged with a servile reverence, betrayed her submission to the radiant presence before her. She signaled to the six converts at the headland to hold their silence.

"Great Mother," Igho's voice trembled with a mix of excitement and fear. "Urgent matters concerning your children... the very reasons for our call."

Ogidigbo's grin widened, a silent acknowledgment of the gravity in Igho's words, as the night's suspense thickened, enveloping the lake in an ominous stillness.

Igho scattered a lavish handful of white powder over the lake's surface, watching as it dissolved into ripples that spread with the subtle thrash of Ogidigbo's massive fin. A faint smile touched her lips as she spoke softly into the night, "Mother of all mothers, a child's cry is a mother's discomfort."

The wind whispered through the trees, tugging at the loose ends of her white cotton wrapper. Ignoring the chill that crept up her spine, Igho sprayed a generous amount of cologne into the air, the sharp scent cutting through the dampness that hung over the lake. With a measured reverence, she picked up a few bottles of soft drinks from the semi-muddy ground and threw them into the lake. The bottles sank quickly, and a loud gurgling sound bubbled up from the lake's depths, shattering the night's fragile silence.

She scattered sachets of biscuits over the water's surface. The fish beneath began a frenzied dance, their quick movements sending small waves across the lake as Ogidigbo's fin gently thrashed.

A gust of wind whipped across the lake, causing her wrapper to billow wildly. Igho's teeth clenched together like grinding metal, the cold seeping into her bones. She grabbed the flailing fabric and wrapped it tighter around her waist, tucking her white blouse securely into the folds.

Her eyes flicked toward the headland where six candles flickered weakly against the relentless wind. Their flames wavered, threatening to extinguish, but somehow, they clung to life. The scent of cologne still lingered in the air, mingling with the biting cold that gnawed at the edges of her resolve.

"I'm but a humble maid at your service," Igho said, treading with caution. "Many are the plaintiff cries of your children. We wish that you would grant us favors."

"Favors. Favors." Ogidigbo grumbled. "Favors don't come cheap."

Ogidigbo vanished beneath the lake's surface, leaving only a web of ripples where she had been. Igho stood paralyzed, her breath catching in her throat.

"Please, don't go, Great Mother! We came with the right sacrifices!" Her voice wavered, eyes shimmering before dimming as they skimmed over the tranquil waters and landed on the three women and two men behind her. Clad only in their pants, they knelt in solemn anticipation, the flickering flames of their candles casting eerie shadows over their bare skin.

The silence was suffocating, broken only by the soft lapping of the lake against the shore. Igho's heart pounded as she fought to find her voice, the gravity of the moment pressing down on her.

"Great Mother," she finally called out, her voice trembling yet resolute. "I plead for your compassion as a child of the realm! Please, come back to us!"

The lake stirred. Ogidigbo emerged slowly, her form shimmering like a specter from the depths. Her caudal fin flicked, sending ripples that danced across the water. She loomed over them, her presence both majestic and terrifying. "Speak then," she commanded, her voice carrying the weight of the ages.

Igho's lips parted, and her voice split the night air with a solemn melody:

Embers in time. Your touch kindles our flames.

Smile and we live, cry and we die. Mother of the sphere.

What's a breath without water? Does life give meaning without breath?

Come, Mother, kindle our flames. We're but embers in your hearth.

We've come to drink from your fountains, Mother of all Mothers.

Ogidigbo swayed in rhythm, her slow, deliberate movements rocking the lake's surface. Igho's hands clapped, her feet pounded the earth, lost in the feverish trance of the song. The six converts joined her, their voices rising in a desperate, almost frenzied harmony:

Embers in time. Your touch kindles our flames.

Smile and we live, cry and we die. Mother of the sphere.

What's a breath without water? Does life give meaning without breath?

Come, Mother, kindle our flames. We're but embers in your hearth.

We've come to drink from your fountains, Mother of all Mothers.

Ogidigbo's smile was faint but unmistakable, the song's power tugging at her ancient heart.

Igho whirled around, her gaze locking onto one of the men. His hands shook as he held a bleating goat against his chest, its fear mirroring their own. She stepped forward, gripping the animal by the horns and pulling it close.

"This is your son's offering," Igho declared, her voice steady, yet laced with desperation. She dragged the goat closer to the water's edge, its bleats growing louder. "Mother, accept it in good faith!"

Igho's hands moved with practiced precision as she poured a thick layer of powder over the goat's trembling head. The white dust settled on its fur like ash, followed by the sharp scent of cologne that stung the night air. She glanced at the young man beside her, nodding for him to lift the animal. His muscles strained, the goat's size proving more cumbersome than he anticipated.

"Help him," Igho ordered, her voice cutting through the stillness. The second man rushed to assist, their combined strength enough to hoist the goat high. It thrashed and bleated, its terror palpable, but they held firm, unyielding. With a grunt, they sent the animal flying through the air. It twisted in the dim light, a dark shape against the inky sky, before plunging into the lake with a muted splash. The water swallowed it whole, leaving only ripples to mark the sacrifice.

Silence reclaimed the night, the surface of the lake smoothing over as if nothing had disturbed it. Ogidigbo's grin widened, her eyes gleaming with a mix of satisfaction and compassion. She glided closer to the shore, her hair shimmering in the moonlight, each strand moving as though alive—a thousand serpents dancing to an ancient rhythm.

"Daughter of the realm," Ogidigbo's voice resonated with the weight of ages, each word laced with the allure of forgotten magic. "I am Ogidigbo, mother of worlds. You've pleased me greatly. Speak your desire, and I shall grant it. Nothing escapes my sight."

Igho's heart pounded as she steadied her voice. "Netu seeks liberty, Great Mother."

"Liberty?" Ogidigbo's eyes narrowed, the word heavy with possibilities. "From what?"

"From the powers of darkness that hold him back, hindering his progress."

A deep, throaty grunt rumbled from Ogidigbo. "I understand. This is no great challenge."

"Thank you, Mother!" Relief softened Igho's voice, her faith unwavering. "You've never failed me."

"A star boy," Ogidigbo mused, her smile widening. "Unjustly bound. I find myself fond of him."

Igho's face lit up, her tone reverent. "I am forever at your service, Mother. It is done, then?"

"And the others?" Ogidigbo's gaze drifted to the kneeling figures, curiosity piqued. "What do they seek?"

"The usual requests, Mother," Igho replied, her voice steady. "Children, protection, success in business, wealth, employment. You know their needs better than I."

"Good," Ogidigbo purred. "Now, cleanse them. Let them bathe in the lake's waters."

With a nod, Igho turned to the six converts. They rose from their knees, each holding a bar of soap and a raffia sponge. Igho sprinkled them with more powder and doused them in cologne, the ritual precise and deliberate. Some stripped bare, others left their pants on, but all stepped into the lake's cool embrace, the water clinging to their skin like a second layer. They scrubbed and splashed, the sounds of their prayers mingling with the gentle lapping of the lake. The night pushed on, timeless and unyielding.

Ogidigbo observed from the shore, her gaze lingering on the makeshift lake formed by the sands of the dry season. She knew its life was brief, destined to vanish once the rains returned and the river reclaimed its territory. But for now, it served its purpose—a sacred space where Igho's faith and dedication could be tested and renewed year after year.

Ogidigbo's eyes narrowed as she watched Igho at the water's edge, her maid washing herself from a plastic bucket filled with the lake's water. A smile tugged at the corners of Ogidigbo's lips. Igho had proven faithful once again.

~ ~ ~

"Hurry, everyone!" Igho called, urgency thick in her voice. "We must return to the shrine before it's too late."

"Just a moment!" Igho replied, scrambling up the lake's bank to the headland.

The moonlight cast Igho in an ethereal glow, her white blouse and wrapper blending with her powdered skin, making her appear like a spectral figure. A sweet, floral scent wafted from her perfumed body, mingling with the night air and teasing Ogidigbo's senses.

Around them, the others rushed through their prayers, tossing raffia sponges and soap into the lake. Shivering from the cold bite of the water and the relentless wind, they clambered up the headland, hands fumbling as they quickly dressed.

As Netu joined Igho, he leaned in close. "Did it go well?"

Igho's lips curved into a smile. "Ogidigbo appeared tonight."

"She did?"

"Yes, and she was pleased with your aura and offerings."

A slow grin spread across Netu's face. "So I'm blessed?"

"You didn't see her? Shimmering in the lake?"

"I didn't."

"No matter," Igho said, her voice low and reassuring. "Your prayers were heard."

They set off toward the village, a single file of silent figures, torchlights cutting through the darkness. The path was narrow, lined with puddles where toads croaked ominously. The foul stench of filth clung to the air as they sidestepped it, but the soft glow of the moon on their powdered faces and white garments gave them an eerie presence, like spirits haunting the night.

Osuowei

Morning sunlight crept over the sleepy Abadama village, casting a warm glow on Ebimi's farm. The cassava stalks, once fragile saplings, now stood tall, their emerald leaves quivering in the breeze. Dark veins bulge from the earth, pulsing with a strange energy.

Ebimi approached, her hoe balanced on her shoulder, a blue basin perched atop her head. Her ebony complexion glistened under the sun, each curve of her figure accentuated by the loose, worn fabric that clung to her. Her dark braids swayed gently with each step, contrasting sharply with the faded colors of her poverty-stricken farmer's clothes. Her deep blue eyes, a striking anomaly against her ebony skin, flickered with intensity as they scanned the clearing. She paused, her breath catching in her throat, as she took in the transformed landscape.

There was a power in her gaze, the kind that bore into the soul, yet it was tinged with disbelief. The anticipation in the air pressed down on her like a weight, and her fast-paced thoughts mirrored the rapid beat of her heart. The silence of the morning was broken only by the soft rustle of leaves, as if the earth itself was whispering secrets just out of reach. Her legs trembled slightly on the narrow path, but she stood firm, her gaze searching for an explanation that simply wasn't there.

As she turned to flee, a soft whisper caressed her ears, "Fear not, sweet one, for you are never alone." The voice was like a gentle brook, its melody weaving through the air.

A resplendent bird, its plumage a dazzling fusion of black, yellow, and white, watched over her from its lofty perch, a beacon of hope amidst the verdant foliage. Its gentle cooing wove a spell of boundless joy, and Ebimi's heart swelled with courage.

With the bird's gentle cooing still resonating in her heart, Ebimi summoned a deep breath and stepped into the transformed farm. The cassava stalks, mere saplings not long ago, now stood tall and robust, their leaves rustling softly in the morning breeze. She approached the nearest plant, her hoe still slung over her shoulder, and gently dug around the base. The earth yielded with ease, revealing a plump, golden tuber. Ebimi's eyes widened as she placed it with care into her enamel basin.

As she harvested a few more tubers, the bird's watchful presence comforted her. The mysterious transformation of her farm, once a struggling plot, now a thriving oasis, felt like a blessing. Ebimi's thoughts swirled with wonder and gratitude.

With her basin filled, Ebimi retreated from the farm, her footsteps light on the narrow path. She hastened home, eager to share the miraculous tale with her husband, Deseiye. As she entered their thatched hut, Deseiye looked up from his morning meal, curiosity etched on his face.

"Ebimi, what's behind that radiant smile?" he asked, his eyes crinkling at the corners.

Ebimi set the basin down, her hands still trembling with excitement. "Come see, Deseiye! Our farm, it's... it's been transformed! I saw it with my own eyes, and a bird spoke to me, telling me not to fear!"

Deseiye's expression changed from curiosity to astonishment as Ebimi recounted her tale. Together, they gazed at the harvested tubers, their hearts filled with wonder and thanksgiving for the mysterious blessing that had befallen their humble farm.

Ebimi's enthusiasm was contagious, and Deseiye's curiosity grew with each passing moment. "Tell me more, Ebimi. What exactly did this bird say?" he asked, his eyes sparkling with intrigue.

Ebimi hesitated, as if unsure how much to reveal. "It just... told me not to fear. That I'm never alone. And then I saw the farm, Deseiye! It's like nothing I've ever seen before. The cassava stalks are so tall and green, and the tubers... oh, the tubers are huge!"

Deseiye's brow furrowed, his mind racing with questions. "That's strange. I've never heard of a bird speaking to anyone before. And what do you mean by 'the farm'? Did someone help you with the harvest?"

Ebimi shook her head, her eyes wide with excitement. "No, no one was there. I swear, Deseiye, it's like the land itself has been blessed. You have to see it for yourself."

Deseiye's curiosity was now a burning fire. He had to see this miraculous farm for himself. "Alright, let's go. I want to see what's going on."

Ebimi hesitated for a brief moment. Then nodded and sashayed away in the direction of the farm with Deseiye on her heels.

As they walked towards the farm, the air grew thick with anticipation. Ebimi's words had painted a vivid picture in Deseiye's mind, and he couldn't shake off the feeling that something extraordinary was waiting for them.

Upon arriving at the farm, Deseiye's eyes scanned the landscape, taking in the towering cassava stalks and the vibrant green leaves. But as he looked closer, his gaze fell upon something that made his heart skip a beat. The tubers, once bulging from the earth, were now gone. In their place stood neat stacks of harvested cassava, waiting to be carted away.

Deseiye's mind reeled as he turned to Ebimi. "What in the world...? Who could have done this?"

Ebimi's face was a mask of confusion. "I told you, Deseiye, I didn't do it. And I didn't see anyone else around."

The air was heavy with suspense as Deseiye approached the stacks, his eyes scanning the surrounding area for any sign of life. But there was none. Just the rustling of leaves and the distant call of a bird, echoing through the stillness.

"Let's take this harvest home," Deseiye said. "And then we'll try to make sense of this miracle."

As they loaded the cassava onto the makeshift sled, Deseiye couldn't shake the unsettling sensation that they were being watched. Unseen eyes seemed to linger in the shadows, waiting for their next move. His spine prickled with a jolt of fear and awe—fear from the eerie, inexplicable presence that loomed around them, and awe from the unnerving belief that their actions were touching something otherworldly.

The journey back home was silent, each lost in their own thoughts. But as they approached their hut, Deseiye turned to Ebimi with a determined look. "We'll get to the bottom of this, Ebimi. Mark my words."

And with that, the mysterious tale of the transformed farm and the whispering bird became a burning quest for truth, one that would change the course of their lives forever.

~ ~ ~

The next day, Ediseiye ventured back to his raffia palms, his heart pounding with eager anticipation. The miracle of the previous day still danced in his memory like a vivid dream. As he neared the palm trees deep within the heart of the rainforest, he spotted something extraordinary: the calabash jug suspended beneath the hole he'd bored into one of the trees brimmed with frothy palm wine, bubbling over with unprecedented abundance. With a mix of awe and excitement, he tapped the other trees, eager to discover what other marvels awaited. The kegs filled at an astonishingly rapid rate.

Meanwhile, Ebimi worked on her farm at the village's edge, her hands moving with a renewed sense of purpose. The cassava tubers seemed to grow before her eyes faster than the normal, their vibrant green leaves reaching for the sky like outstretched arms each new day. She harvested the tubers a few days later with a sense of wonder, the yield surpassing their wildest expectations.

As the days passed, their prosperity grew, and they became the toast of the village. The local gin distilled from the palm wine sold for a handsome price at the market, and the cassava tubers became the envy of everyone in the village. Their once-humble hut transformed into a thriving enterprise, with customers flocking from afar to taste their miraculous gin and savour their succulent cassava.

But amidst the prosperity, Ediseiye's mind began to stir with unease. He couldn't shake off the feeling that their wealth came with a price, that some unseen force was orchestrating their success. He questioned himself inwardly, *"What could be the source of this bounty? Is it mere coincidence or something more sinister?"*

As the nights wore on, Ediseiye's discomfort grew. He would lie awake, his mind racing with thoughts of the whispering bird his wife hinted of, the transformed farm, and the raffia palms' miraculous yield.

Ebimi, sensing his unease, would reassure him, "We're blessed, Ediseiye. We've worked hard for this. The gods favor us."

But Ediseiye couldn't shake off the feeling that they were mere pawns in a larger game, that their prosperity was a mere illusion. The suspense gnawed at him, threatening to unravel the very fabric of their newfound happiness.

~ ~ ~

In the heart of Ebimi's dreamscape, a tempest materialized with an almost tangible force. From the swirling mists emerged Osuowei, an apparition so striking he seemed born from the very essence of the night itself. His face, a masterpiece of sharp lines and high cheekbones, radiated a fierce allure, while his eyes—brilliant, mischievous—held the glint of ancient mischief, as if they had witnessed ages beyond reckoning.

A familiar portrait of her recent dreams.

She reckoned his skin, glowing with a sunlit warmth, contrasted sharply with his untamed black hair, a wild cascade of strands adorned with feathers and tiny shining flecks that whispered in the dream's breeze. His perpetual smile, a sly curl of lips, hinted at enigmas too profound for mortal minds.

Osuowei was draped in a robe of flowing white, its fabric shimmering like moonlight on water. The robe was cinched with a belt of shadow, its form shifting and undulating with an elusive darkness. Around his neck, an ethereal pendant pulsed softly, casting an eerie luminescence that danced across the shifting dreamscape, weaving threads of mystery into the fabric of the night.

As he moved, his presence seemed to shift and ripple, like the surface of a pond disturbed by a thrown stone. His voice was low and husky, with a hint of a growl, sending shivers down Ebimi's spine.

Despite his fearsome aspect, Osuowei exuded an aura of dark allure, drawing Ebimi in with an irresistible force. His eyes seemed to hold a deep wisdom, a knowledge of secrets and mysteries that only the gods could fathom.

In his presence, Ebimi felt both thrilled and terrified, like a leaf caught in a storm's vortex. She knew that Osuowei was a force beyond her control, a deity who commanded respect and inspired awe. And yet, she felt an inexplicable connection to him, as if their fates were intertwined by threads of destiny.

"Ebimi, daughter of the land," Osuowei's voice boomed, "your gratitude is due. Raise an altar of white linen and white porcelain, and offer native kola nuts and Fanta as propitiation."

Ebimi's dream self nodded, and upon waking, she felt an unshakeable sense of purpose. She went about the task she'd been given almost immediately and constructed the altar with reverence, placing the offerings with precision.

As the days passed, their fortunes skyrocketed. Customers flocked to their gin and cassava stalls, and their wealth grew exponentially. But amidst the prosperity, a storm brewed.

Deseiye's eyes narrowed as he beheld the altar one afternoon. "Ebimi, what sorcery is this? We're Christians, not pagans!"

Ebimi's voice remained calm, but her heart raced. "It's just a token of gratitude, Deseiye. Osuowei appeared to me in a dream—"

"Osuowei?" Deseiye's tone turned incredulous. "You mean that ancient deity? Ebimi, have you forgotten our Lord and Savior?"

The argument escalated, their voices clashing like thunder.

"I'm not forgetting anyone, Deseiye! This is about acknowledging the source of our blessings!"

"Source? You mean some heathen god? I won't have it, Ebimi!"

The air was heavy with tension as they stood, faces inches apart, their words hanging like daggers.

Then, in an instant, the storm dissipated. Deseiye's expression softened, and he looked upon Ebimi with a mix of confusion and concern.

"Ebimi, my love, what's happening to us? I feel like we're losing ourselves in all this."

Ebimi's shoulders sagged, her voice faint. "I don't know, Deseiye. But I feel it too."

The altar, once a symbol of gratitude, now stood as a testament to their discord. The kola nuts and Fanta seemed to mock them, a reminder of the unknown forces driving their lives.

~ ~ ~

After three days of restless contemplation, Ediseiye approached the altar, his hands trembling. The weight of his decision overwhelming him, intensified by the lingering fog of a binge on *ogogoro* with friends at the local drinking joint. His heart thudded with a heavy sense of foreboding, each step toward the altar echoing his inner turmoil. The evening sun cast long shadows, like skeletal fingers, across the room. He glanced around with nervous attention, ensuring Ebimi was nowhere in sight. With a swift motion, he gathered the offerings - kola nuts, Fanta, and white linen - and shoved them into a sack. *I know where this belongs. In the river, not here*, he swore inwardly, rushing out of the house.

~ ~ ~

On return from her market stall that day, Ebimi's woven basket thudded to the ground, the plantains and dried fish spilling across the cemented floor. The room, usually filled with the scent of burning incense and the soft glow of candlelight, now felt cold, as though life had drained from it. Her heart pounded as she stepped closer to the empty space where her altar once stood. The flickering candles, the sacred incense, the offerings—all gone. Only the small stool where she'd placed these items remained, mocking her devotion. Her throat choked a scream.

The door creaked behind her at that moment, and she spun around to find Ediseiye standing in the doorway, his face a mask of guilt and fear. His breath came in ragged gasps, reeking of *ogogoro* and his eyes darted around the room, avoiding hers.

"What have you done?" Ebimi's voice wavered, but the weight of her words struck him like a blow.

Ediseiye swallowed hard, his mouth dry. "I—I had to, Ebimi. It was the only way..."

"The only way?" Her voice rose, laced with disbelief. "The only way to what? To ruin us? To bring the wrath of the gods upon this house?"

A gust of wind rattled the window shutters, filling the silence that hung between them like a knife's edge. Ediseiye took a hesitant step forward, but Ebimi held up her hand, stopping him in his tracks.

"I had no choice," he pleaded, his voice breaking. "They said—"

"I don't care what they said!" Ebimi cut him off, her anger flaring. "Osuowei has protected this family and brought good fortune. You've condemned us, Ediseiye!"

Tears welled in Ediseiye's eyes as he fell to his knees, his hands trembling. "Forgive me, Ebimi. I thought I was saving us."

Ebimi's gaze burned into him, her chest tightening with fear and sorrow. "You've done the opposite," she whispered, her words thick with dread. "You've opened a door that should have remained shut."

The room seemed to darken, shadows creeping along the walls as if the very spirit she had worshipped now watched from the corners, silent and enraged. A heavy silence pressed down on them, the import of their actions settling like a curse.

Ebimi's hand reached instinctively to her waist band, where her special coin given to her by Osuowei used to be. But it was gone, just like the altar. She took a step back, her breath shallow and quick, as if the air itself had turned against her.

Outside, the wind howled, and the river that had carried away their fate roared louder than ever, as if mocking the desperation that now filled the space between husband and wife.

Ediseiye's expression was resolute, but his eyes betrayed a glimmer of fear. "I won't have pagan rituals in our home, Ebimi."

Ebimi's days blurred into a haze of defeat. Each morning, she watched the raffia palms in the forest, once heavy with sweet sap, standing limp, their trunks twisted and leaves browned like corpses under the sun. She touched the dry earth beneath her bare feet, once alive with the promise of cassava roots. Now, the plants curled at the edges, thirsting for something beyond water. The air was thick with the absence of their fortunes; the village no longer whispered her name with envy.

At home, she knelt before Osuowei's altar, her forehead pressed to the ground. The offerings—the Fanta, the biscuits, the kola nuts, the candies—lay untouched. Ebimi whispered her pleas into the silence. The air felt still, as though the deity's ears were deaf to her cries. When she rose, her knees trembled, not from devotion, but from the weight of unanswered prayers.

The once-lively market square where her stall was a beehive of activities echoed now with hollowness. Even her native gin, the pride of her husband's craft, sat untouched on the vendor's tables. No buyers, no bartering. Just bottles lined up like forgotten relics of better days.

Then, on that evening when the sun bled into the horizon, Ediseiye stumbled through the door. His breaths were ragged, eyes wide with something far darker than fear. "Ebimi..." His voice broke, the words scratching their way out of his throat. "I've seen him. Osuowei."

She saw it before she understood it—the terror flickering in his eyes, the trembling in his hands. The room seemed to shrink, the air growing thick with his panic. Before she could reach for him, Ediseiye turned, fleeing from their home. His feet pounded against the earth as he ran toward the river, his figure swallowed by the growing night.

Ebimi's screams were drowned out by the sound of rushing water. She rushed to the river, her heart racing, and saw Ediseiye's body floating face down in the river. But as she approached, she saw something that made her blood run cold.

Ediseiye's eyes, seemingly frozen in death throes, now flickered open. He gazed up at Ebimi as she reached and pull him out of the shallow end of the river, his pupils black as coal, and whispered a single word: "Run."

Suddenly, the river began to churn and foam, as if something beneath the surface was stirring. Ebimi stumbled back, horror etched on her face, as Ediseiye's body began to sink beneath the waves.

And then, a hand shot out of the water, grasping for Ebimi's ankle...

ABADAMA-ERE

"DAMN! THE HOUR HAS come..." Abadama-ere's voice trembled that morning, her words barely escaping her lips as she stood frozen on the path. The brief, surreal glimpses of the realm had shattered her composure, flooding her senses with an overwhelming torrent of meanings that she struggled to comprehend. Her legs, like lead, refused to move, anchoring her in place as the weight of the revelation pressed down on her chest.

But as the icy fingers of panic threatened to pull her under, she forced herself to refocus. Her gaze locked onto the vast sea ahead, its surface shrouded in a dense, shifting mist that seemed almost alive, beckoning her closer. The watery haze stirred an instinct deep within her—a dangerous pull that urged her to surrender, to plunge into its enigmatic depths. Yet, with every ounce of willpower she had left, she fought against the compulsion, knowing that losing control now would mean losing herself to the call of the deep.

The mist swirled, thickening, as if aware of her momentary homecoming. The very air seemed to hum with tension, a silent battle between her will and the unrelenting force of the realm. She could feel the sea's cold breath on her skin, the moisture clinging to her like an unwelcome touch. Every nerve in her body screamed to flee, but the pull was too strong, too alluring.

Abadamaere's breath came in sharp gasps as she fought to anchor herself to reality, her heart hammering in her chest. She couldn't afford to lose. Not now. Not here. But as the mist coiled around her like a phantom's touch, she felt its cold fingers grazing her soul, a grim reminder of the duty she could not evade. The realm was on the verge of birthing a new movement—what humans would soon call a church—and as High Priestess, her presence was imperative.

"Give me a moment. I'll be there. Soon as I can," Abadamaere whispered, her voice laced with desperation. Her eyes darted across the shifting shadows, searching for something solid to anchor her to reality. "This is all too sudden," she added, though the words felt hollow, drowned out by the roar of the sea waves that pounded in her ears like a relentless drumbeat. The urge to flee gnawed at her, a primal instinct that tugged at the edges of her sanity, but her legs refused to obey.

She tried to turn away, to break free from the seeming chains that held her fast on the narrow path. The milling crowd pressed in, a faceless sea of bodies at the seashore, their murmurings a low, haunting drone that filled the air with an eerie tension. Panic bubbled up inside her, but when she willed her legs to move, they remained fixed in place, as though rooted to the earth beneath her feet. The crowd's faceless sea of bodies closed in, their murmurs weaving a haunting spell that wrapped around her like a shroud. Panic clawed at her chest, but her legs refused to budge.

Memories of her fervent declarations during service echoed in her mind: "I'll minister in the sea... a new church will rise... I'll return at dusk." Her congregants had scoffed, but now the sea's siren call beckoned her, its whispery voice caressing her spirit like a lover's gentle touch.

The mist swirled, tendrils curling around her ankles like ethereal fingers, drawing her in. The water's hypnotic rhythm pulsed, a heartbeat that synchronized with her own. She felt herself slipping, surrendering to the river's enchantment, her essence entwining with its flow.

The crowd's drone grew louder, a discordant counterpoint to the sea's sweet melody. Abadama-ere's heart wrestled with the conflicting calls, her mission and her mortality hanging in the balance. The mist rose higher, a chilling embrace that threatened to consume her. Would she resist, or succumb to the river's promise?

She fought to resist, to keep her mind clear, but her thoughts grew foggy, tangled in the mesmerizing dance of the sea. The crowd around her seemed to pulse in time with the current, their presence growing more oppressive, more suffocating. Every fiber of her being screamed to run, to escape the grip of the unseen force that tugged at her soul, yet she walked now towards it.

Abadamaere's breath hitched as the mist crept higher, brushing her waist now, its chill seeping into her bones. She tried to resist, to call out for help, but the sound died in her throat, swallowed by the sweet hum of the swirling sea. The water shimmered, beckoning her closer, its depths promising both release and duty.

The battle within her raged, a storm of fear and longing that tore at her mind. She knew she had to make a choice, but the sea's pull was relentless, its song too sweet to ignore. The mist curled around her neck, cold and clammy, as the water ahead churned with anticipation, ready to welcome her whole. The world around her blurred, the crowd fading into shadows, as she teetered on the edge of surrender.

Cries of caution echo upland from the teeming members of her spiritual movement, eager to see what she'll do to resolve this mystery – a mortal's transit in flesh to the realm. She'd least expected the realm's call, yet the new movement must rise there. There's entreaty from the milling crowd for her not to get closer to the seashore, yet she must obey its command if she wants the puzzle solved. So, she walked entranced towards the sea, stopping once in a while to look at the audience, waving at them not to worry that she would be safe at the end.

Abadama-ere's white silk gown, adorned with intricate embroidery on the lapels and cape, caught the wind as she approached the sea's edge. The fabric fluttered like wings, the hemline brushing against her ankles as she stepped into the cool water. With a deliberate grip, she held the gown's edges, wading in deeper, the water now swirling around her knees. She paused, casting a glance over her shoulder—whether to heed the warnings or bask in the silent cheers from the onlookers, it was unclear. But her gaze was resolute.

Without hesitation, Abadama-ere placed the flag of her church, which she'd been holding all along at the shoreline, then moved further into the panning waves, the water rising to claim her. The spectators held their breath as the seashore swelled, its waves seeming to rush forward, eager to embrace her. Then, in a heartbeat, she vanished beneath the surface, leaving only ripples that danced on the water's surface—a fleeting echo of her presence, swallowed by the sea's unrelenting current.

A piercing shriek cut through the air, drawing every eye to Abadama-ere's mother, her frail frame trembling as she stood by the shoreline. Her wrinkled hands clawed at her tear-soaked face, trying to stem the flood of grief, but it was a losing battle. The weight of loss crushed her spirit, and she collapsed onto the damp sand, her cries mingling with the crashing waves.

A few of Abadama-ere's aides dashed forward, lifting her limp body from the cold, wet ground. Her eyes, red and swollen, bore the agony of a mother's heartbreak. She clung to life, but barely, as the pain threatened to pull her under.

Feet rooted in the sand, the crowd watched as ripples faded in slow motion on the sea's surface, where Abadama-ere had vanished. Eyes widened, lips quivered, yet no sound escaped. The sea's relentless current churned on, indifferent to the eyes searching for a sign, any sign of life. A child clutched her mother's skirt, the fabric twisting under her tiny, desperate grip. Shadows lengthened across the shore, the sun dimming as if mourning with them. No one shifted, no one whispered—the weight of loss pressed against their chests, tightening with each passing moment. The wind, once playful, now carried only the scent of damp earth and the silent promise of sorrow.

~ ~ ~

Minutes stretched into hours, each one slipping by with relentless speed. The seashore, once calm, now churned and foamed, mirroring the turmoil etched on the faces of the crowd. Eyes, heavy with worry and fear, burned under the weight of grief, their tears mingling with the dusk. The wails of loved ones and converts had dwindled to a subdued murmur, their voices lost amid the encroaching night.

As the sun dipped below the horizon, painting the sky with a surreal, shifting glow, the surface of the shoreline began to writhe. The shore twisted with sudden turbulence, sending ripples that glowed with an eerie luminescence. From the depths, a figure emerged, shrouded in a ghostly light, rising in slow motion as if drawn by unseen hands. The crowd gasped, their eyes widening, the air charged with a mixture of dread and disbelief. A profound silence fell, the sky's vibrant hues now a haunting backdrop to the enigmatic apparition before them.

Against the deepening dusk, Abadama-ere's figure emerged from the encroaching shadows, pristine and enigmatic, like a specter risen from the abyss. Her teeth, catching the fleeting light of twilight, glistened like scattered diamonds as she grinned widely, surveying the mournful procession at the shoreline. Clad in her white silk gown that swept to her ankles, it remained untouched by the dampness of the sea. To her daughter, Tama, who had first glimpsed her from a distance, Abadama-ere seemed to have grown taller and darker in the brief hours of her absence. Her smile, though warm, was tinged with an unsettling mystery, mirroring the enigmatic aura that had shrouded her when she vanished beneath the waves.

Her steps towards the sandy shore flowed with an otherworldly grace, each motion a silent symphony, as though the twilight air itself reverberated with the soft chime of distant bells. Her hips swayed rhythmically, her head tilted in an almost ceremonial gesture, and a smile—both radiant and shrouded in mystery—danced on her lips. In her delicate hands, an object glowed with an unspoken promise, hinting at a transformation born from the depths and a tale meant only for her to reveal—one that whispered of distant realms and untold secrets.

The atmosphere exploded with jubilant cries as the crowd recognized Abadama-ere, their voices a cacophony of excitement. Tama, her beloved nineteen-year-old daughter, surged forward, arms outstretched and a cry of joy on her lips. Yet, as she neared, Abadama-ere's hand lifted in a subtle, commanding gesture—a silent decree of "not yet." Her eyes, still veiled in the shadows of her mission, conveyed an unspoken message: the journey was not yet complete.

Abadama-ere climbed the upland, her eyes scanning the throng with intense urgency. "Where is Bralade?" she demanded, her voice cutting through the murmur of the crowd. When at last her gaze locked onto him navigating the sea of jubilant faces, she moved swiftly, gripping his trembling hand with a fierce determination.

Her other hand clutched a bright, ornate object. She pressed it to his forehead, and he flinched, his face paling as if the very life was being drained from him. He staggered, but Abadama-ere's firm grip prevented him from collapsing. She held her smile steady, her eyes gleaming with a triumphant fire.

The upland air was thick with the scent of earth and sweat as her voice cut through the jubilant chaos, resonating with a blend of pride and relief. "It's done!" she declared, her words carrying the weight of victory, rippling through the crowd that buzzed with unbridled celebration. Her hand, steady yet commanding, gestured towards the distant offices, a hint of something more lurking just beyond the horizon.

"There's more to come over there," she added, a subtle promise that sent a ripple of anticipation through the throng. The man beside her moved, not of his own accord but as if drawn by an unseen force, his steps faltering as if he were being led into uncharted territory. The crowd surged behind them, voices rising in a fevered chant, a medley of melodies that blended into the hum of suspense.

~ ~ ~

Abadama-ere's brown eyes, sharp as embers in a dying fire, scanned the gathering crowd with a gaze that seemed to pierce through to their very souls. There was a distant, almost dreamlike quality to her stare, as if she were seeing beyond the present moment. She lowered herself into the plush white seat with a thud that threatened to unseat it from its very foundation, her weight sinking into the fabric like a stone into water. The auditorium, vast and echoing, was filling quickly, the air charged with the tension of anticipation. Her round white cap tipped precariously to one side as her gaze fixed on a young man elbowing his way to the front row, desperation etched in every line of his face.

"Come forward, Akpoebi," Abadama-ere's voice boomed, her spindly finger pointing at him like an arrow. The room seemed to hold its breath as she continued, her tone heavy with foreboding. "The goddess has revealed the source of your troubles. Look no further—the rat gnawing at your toe is also blowing it with sweet air." The words hung in the air, heavy with the weight of revelation, as the crowd shifted uneasily, caught between belief and doubt, each of them silently wondering what secrets might be unearthed next.

The Aziza Priest

Papa Johnson Udze hobbled down the narrow street with his bow legs, his single good eye scanning the dim path ahead. The air hung thick with the scent of burnt wood, an omen of the calamity that awaited him. He quickened his pace, his heart pounding with an unfamiliar urgency. When he turned the corner to his street, the site ahead stopped him dead in his tracks.

The skeletal remains of what used to be their rented two-bedroom in a mini-estate at Odu Road, Warri loomed against the orange glow of the setting sun. Smoke curled from the charred wood, spiraling into the sky as if it sought to join the spirits above. Papa Udze's knees buckled. The house he had left that morning with his wife, Onome, inside was now a ruin.

His fingers trembled as he placed his right hand on his chest—a supplication to the Aziza deity he had served with unwavering devotion for decades. But now, standing before the remnants of his life, he felt the cold tendrils of doubt creep into his heart.

"Who did this?" he croaked, his voice barely audible over the crackling of the dying embers.

A small crowd had gathered around the perimeter of the building, their faces etched with curiosity and pity. An old woman, his neighbor, her back bent with age, stepped forward. "It was Onome, your wife," she said, her voice laced with sorrow. "She lit a fire that spread through the house...and then she ran."

Papa Udze's good eye widened in disbelief. "Onome? But why?" His mind raced, trying to piece together the events that had led to this disaster. Onome was a gentle soul, not given to acts of destruction. Yet here he was, staring at the ruin she had wrought due to the little quarrel over food allowance they had the previous night.

Before he could process the weight of her betrayal, the sound of heavy boots crunching on gravel drew his attention. A group of policemen, led by the landlord, emerged from the crowd. The landlady, a stout woman with a perpetually furrowed brow, pointed an accusatory finger at Papa Udze.

"You!" the landlady barked. "You're responsible for this! Your wife has fled, and now you'll answer for her crime."

Papa Udze had little or no time to protest before the policemen seized him. The iron grip of their hands on his frail arms sent a wave of fear through his body. They hauled him away, his protests drowned out by the murmurs of the crowd.

In the small, dimly lit cell at the police station, Papa Udze sat on a bare floor with a dozen people arrested for various offenses, his head bowed in despair. The walls felt as though they were closing in on him, the air thick with the stench of sweat and fear. His fingers fumbled with chest again, seeking solace in the symbol of the deity he had served so faithfully.

Aziza, he prayed silently, *where are you? Have you abandoned me too?*

The night was unusually still. The air was laden with the stench from the toilet bucket at the far right corner, and the promise of a storm, but no wind stirred the leaves. Papa Udze sat crouched at the corner of his darkened cell, his eye closed in prayer, hands clasped tight around his bare chest. The cell's cold stone walls seemed to press in on him, narrowing his world to the steady, rhythmic sound of his breathing and the snores from his cell mates and the faint drip of water from somewhere deep within the station.

A faint rumble of thunder rolled in the distance, but it felt more like a growl than a warning. The single flickering bulb overhead cast long, shifting shadows, making the cell feel like a cage for something far more dangerous than the old priest could fathom.

A sudden chill pricked Papa Johnson Udze's spine, forcing a shiver through him. The cell froze, colder than it had been all night. He opened his eyes, blinking into the darkness and squinting as he tried to see past the shadows. Heat began to tingle in the center of his left palm, growing hotter against his skin. His breath hitched.

Then came the whispers.

Low, guttural sounds that slithered from the corners of the room, a language older than the stones of the cell itself. The shadows seemed to pulse in response, growing larger, darker, until they filled the space with an oppressive, almost suffocating presence. Papa Udze's heart pounded, its pulse now almost doubling by the seconds. He knew what this was. He had served long enough to recognize the signs.

"Aziza..." he breathed, but his voice was lost in the cacophony of snores and groaning that filled the room. The shadows converged, swirling into a single form that towered over him, its outline hardly discernible in the dim light.

A pair of glowing eyes snapped open in the darkness, fixing on him with a gaze that felt like it pierced straight through to his soul. The whispers stopped, the silence that followed more terrifying than the noise.

"Papa Udze," the figure intoned, its voice a rumble of thunder that shook the walls of the cell. "You have called, and I have answered."

The priest's knees buckled, and he sank to the floor, bowing his head in reverence. "Aziza, forgive me. I am unworthy…"

The figure took a step forward, side-stepping the sea of naked bodies on the floor, the ground trembling under its weight. "You are my servant, and you have been wronged. The balance must be restored."

A flash of lightning illuminated the cell, and for a brief moment, Papa Udze saw the full form of Aziza. The deity was magnificent, his presence commanding, draped in robes of shimmering water that seemed to flow around him like a living river. His eyes blazed with an inner fire, and his face—though human in shape—was marked by the features of a force of nature, untamed and eternal.

"You have been faithful, Papa Udze," Aziza continued, his voice softening, though it lost none of its power. "But those who have wronged you have not. The house shall be restored, and your name cleared. But first…"

Aziza's form shifted, the water around him swirling in a vortex of energy. "The one who caused this pain must be found. Onome… she shall not escape."

The name hung in the air like a curse. Papa Udze felt a pang of sorrow, but he knew better than to plead for mercy. Aziza's justice was as swift as it was certain, and Onome's betrayal could not go unanswered. He kept his head bowed, feeling the weight of the deity's gaze upon him.

Aziza extended a hand, the air around it crackling with energy. "You shall see it done, Udze. She is beyond my direct reach, but not yours."

Before Papa Udze could respond, the deity stepped back, his form beginning to fade into the shadows. "Return home," Aziza commanded, his voice already growing distant. "You will find things… different."

With that, Aziza vanished, leaving Papa Udze alone in the cell, the only sound the pounding of his own heart and the distant echo of thunder.

With a wave of his hand, Aziza summoned forth his retinue of artisans and craftsmen from the water realm. They appeared one by one, their forms shimmering like the surface of a moonlit river. Without a word, they departed, leaving behind the cell that now felt empty without Aziza's presence.

~ ~ ~

Two days later, the dawn broke with a suddenness that startled the landlady. She had barely closed her eyes when the sound of hammers and saws began to echo down the street. She rushed outside, only to see a miraculous sight—the burned house, once a ruin, was being rebuilt with impossible speed. Artisans in all white gear worked with supernatural precision, their movements a blur. Within a week, the house stood tall once more, a pristine structure where chaos had reigned just few days before.

But it wasn't just the house. The artisans compensated every tenant who had lost property in the fire—new cars replaced burnt ones, lost money was returned, and goods that had been reduced to ashes were miraculously restored.

By the time the sun reached its zenith on the seventh day, the work was done. The artisans vanished as quickly as they had come, leaving the neighborhood in stunned silence.

That afternoon, the landlady received an unexpected visitor. Aziza, now in human form, stood before her, his presence radiating an aura of quiet menace. The landlady, her bravado gone, cowered under the deity's gaze.

"You dare to imprison my servant over your house?" Aziza's voice was calm, but it carried the weight of an ocean's fury. "Know this, mortal—he is under my protection. Harm him again, and your fate will be sealed."

The landlady, trembling, fell to her knees. "Forgive me!" she cried, her voice breaking. "I had no idea..."

Aziza's eyes narrowed. "You are forgiven, but remember—my wrath is not easily appeased."

With that, Aziza turned and left, leaving the landlady in a heap on the floor, her heart pounding with the terror of what she had narrowly escaped.

~ ~ ~

The next morning, the police station was abuzz with nervous energy. The officers avoided Papa Udze's gaze as they led him out, their faces pale and drawn. Something had happened during the night, something that none of them could explain, but the whispers had already started—stories of strange noises, of unnatural cold, of shadows that moved with a mind of their own.

The landlady too had come to the station to seek his immediate release without pressing further charges. Her withdrawal of the case seemed hasty and induced by something extrasensory. When Papa Udze stepped out into the morning light, he found the street deserted, the usual bustle of the market stilled by an uneasy silence. It was as if the city of Warri itself was holding its breath, waiting for something terrible to happen.

With each step, the weight of what awaited him pressed down on his shoulders. When he reached the house, he halted, his breath catching. The ruins he'd left behind were gone. In their place stood a structure restored to its former glory—every beam straight, every window intact. But the air around it was thick, oppressive, as though the house had severed itself from the world.

Papa Udze stood in the doorway, his hand on the polished wood. The house stood tall, a miracle in itself, yet something about it made his skin crawl. As he stepped inside, the scent of incense, rich and heady, mingled with the salty tang of the sea. Shadows danced across the floor, their movements exaggerated by the slivers of sunlight that filtered through the covered windows.

And there she was.

Onome sat bound in the center of the room, her eyes wide with fear. When she saw him, her breath hitched, a desperate plea spilling from her lips. "Udze... please... you have to believe me..."

Papa Udze's heart tightened, but he kept his voice steady. "Onome," he said, quiet but firm. "Why did you do it?"

She shook her head, tears streaming down her cheeks. "It wasn't me! I swear it wasn't me! I didn't mean to... I don't even know how it happened!"

The words came out in a rush, but Papa Udze could see the truth in her eyes—she was terrified, and not just of him. Something had driven her to this, something beyond her control.

A low growl echoed through the room, and Onome flinched, her eyes darting to the shadows. "It's here... it's still here... I can feel it..."

Papa Udze stiffened. His heart pulsed with warmth, and he felt a familiar presence—Aziza, watching, waiting. The deity's justice was swift, but it was also patient. Onome's fate was sealed, but first, the truth had to be uncovered.

He knelt beside her, placing a hand on her bound wrists. "Tell me everything," he said softly, "and I will make sure you are safe."

Onome's breath caught, and she nodded, the words spilling out in a desperate whisper. "It was the landlord... he made me do it... he said if I didn't, he'd... he'd..."

The rest of her words were lost in a sob, but Papa Udze understood. The landlord had used her, manipulated her into doing his bidding, and now she was paying the price. But the landlord had underestimated the power of the deity, and that mistake would cost him dearly.

Papa Udze rose to his feet, his resolve hardening. The storm was coming, and there was no stopping it now. The landlord would pay, and Onome's soul would be spared—if she could survive what was to come.

As he stepped back into the shadows, Papa Udze whispered a prayer, not for himself, but for the woman who had once been his wife. Aziza's justice was coming, and the city of Warri would never be the same again.

Eyouror and the Hydra

Lagos, Nigeria, 1973

Eyouror stared at the living room wall, her eyes unblinking. The emissary's message from the white captain of the biggest ocean liner in Nigeria, the Royal ship, weighed on her mind like an asteroid drifting through space, heavy and dangerous. The crew's fate hinged on her decision, a burden even for a revered sorceress like her.

She shifted her gaze to the two men seated before her, feeling the weight of their expectations. They had no idea what they were asking. Did they truly believe the high seas held only fish and water? Secrets swirled beneath the surface, dark and deadly.

Her eyes narrowed as visions of a ship in the high sea flashed in her mind, but she pushed them away. When she looked at the rotund man in the dapper frock, his deep, dark eyes filled with worry, she flinched.

"I'm sorry," she whispered, her voice trembling. "What you ask is too risky. A sea god is angry. You failed to appease him. Mortal danger awaits."

The men shifted in their seats, their eyes wide with fear.

Eyouror glared at them, her frustration boiling over. For two decades, she had served as a medium, never imagining a day like this would come. Why hadn't she objected when the realm bestowed upon her the gift of foresight? But what choice had she really had? They needed a human to bridge the worlds, and she had been chosen. And now, duty called.

"I'll do it. On one condition."

"Name your price, Priestess," the emissary, Ebiri, blurted out. "We'll do anything for the safety of the crew and the ship."

She closed her eyes, the weight of her decision pressing down on her. After years of interceding for humans, confronting elemental beings with astonishing results, she knew there was no escaping this fate. According to Ebiri whom she'd known for some time as a sailor and client, the crew had done everything in their power to steer the ship beyond the iceberg that trapped it on their way back to Nigeria from London, but a dark force held it hostage—a force no engineer or meteorologist could conquer.

Eyouror knew the realm's ways, knew that she alone could turn the sails forward, undo the damage inflicted by the custodian of the deep. Victory or catastrophe—both now hung on her choice.

"We'll do it my way," Eyouror declared, her voice cutting through the tension in the room. "Follow my lead."

Ebiri didn't hesitate. "Consider it done," he replied, eager at the prospect of rescue. "Anything you say, Priestess."

Long before the two men had arrived, whispers of impending doom had filled Eyouror's ears, visions of icebergs rising from the depths, blocking passages and sealing the fate of countless ships. But those glimpses offered no specifics—until the strangers knocked on her door.

That the crew, including the captain and his men, had survived this long was nothing short of a mystery to Eyouror. A new dawn was possible, but only if they followed her guidance, aligning with the sorceress's universe.

The path forward required sacrifice. The cost was huge, yet vital, a price that could secure their freedom. Eyouror knew she could bear the risk, even if it demanded a life.

"I'll go," she said, her voice breaking the silence like a knife. "Yes, I will go with you."

"Is there anything you'll need for the job?" Ebiri asked eagerly. "Whatever it takes, just say so."

"Get these items fast," Eyouror ordered, her tone commanding. "A dozen cartons of sweet biscuits, sardines, crates of Fanta, seven bottles of Seaman's dry gin, packets of candies or sweets. You have 30 minutes."

"How much do we pay for your service?" probed Ebiri.

Eyouror thought for a few seconds. "Sixty thousand Pounds Sterling," she said.

"Is it negotiable?"

"Not at all."

"Alright then," Ebiri conceded. "I'll let the captain know as we proceed."

The men sprang to their feet, thanked her profusely, and rushed out to gather the items.

As the door closed behind them, Eyouror's thoughts spiraled. What if she had refused their call? She longed for freedom from such burdens, to predict the future without physical involvement, to heal the sick with ease, to soar through other realms in her trance flights without a single worry. That priceless freedom—it was all she wanted. It was non-negotiable.

"Be back in time," she called after them, snapping out of her reverie. "Time is ticking."

Silence enveloped the room as she waited, her mind churning. Had she made the right decision? What about her safety, her dreams?

A voice echoed in her ears, cutting through her doubts. "No daughter of ours is given to self-conceit. When duty calls, you answer. Is that not why you were granted such power?"

Eyouror shuddered. That damning voice—there was no escape. Another assignment awaited, whether she liked it or not.

~ ~ ~

The two men from the ship returned swiftly, their footsteps a muffled echo in the silence of her living room. "The items you requested are ready in the car," Ebiri Kobigha announced, his voice tight with anticipation. "It cost us sixty thousand Pound Sterling."

Eyouror's eyes flickered with something unreadable as she nodded. "I knew it would be so considering the gravity of the situation. Contact the captain. Tell him to have his men prepare a makeshift cage, large enough to hold all the supplies, plus four persons. No questions," she ordered, her tone sharp, cutting through the tension in the room. "Are you ready?"

"Yes, ready!" they chorused, snapping to attention. The quieter man pulled out a Thuraya cell phone, his fingers trembling slightly as he relayed her instructions to the ship's captain.

Eyouror rose from her seat, disappearing into her bedroom. Moments later, she emerged, draped in an all-white wrapper and blouse, her skin glistening with a mix of white powder and overpowering cologne. The white lace scarf on her head complemented the small white bag hung from her hand, the paraphernalia of her trade rattling softly inside. "Shall we?' she asked and added in the same breath, "We'll make a detour first at Warri port before heading out to sea."

The men exchanged a quick glance not sure if it was the right thing to do, then nodded, leading her outside. Despite the fact that the trip to Warri was not part of their initial agreement, anything that would aid in rescuing the Royal was most welcome. The car waited a short distance away from Eyouror's house at Ajegunle, Lagos, its engine purring softly, as though aware of the ominous task ahead.

~ ~ ~

At the NPA jetty in Warri four hours later, a medium-sized speed boat rocked gently on the waves, its awning flapping in the sea breeze. The boat's pilot spotted the approaching car and fired up the engine at once, his eyes narrowing with a mix of curiosity and awe.

"They're here," he muttered to his co-pilot, leaning forward as if the motion would bring him closer to the unfolding scene.

The sturdy man, Ebiri, from the ship sprang from the car as it rolled to a stop, his movements quick and precise. He opened the back door with a flourish, bowing deeply as Eyouror stepped out. "This way, Priestess," he said, his voice a low rumble, pointing towards the speedboat that hummed at the waterfront.

A gust of wind lashed across Eyouror's face, carrying the stench of decay—rotting fish and the sharp tang of salt. She wrinkled her nose but said nothing, following the man down the ramp to where the boat bobbed like a restive youth.

The smaller man, with the wiry frame, assisted her onto the boat, then hurried back to the car to load the cartons of biscuits, sardines, and dry gin. The sturdy man stood by, his eyes in nervous flick from the ramp to the boat, and back again. "We're heading out to sea," he said, more to himself than anyone else. "Put on your life jackets."

Eyouror ignored the command, settling into her seat. Her gaze drifted to the water, watching as the currents twisted and turned, brushing against the boat's hull. She reached for a small sachet of chocolate sweets, tearing it open with deliberate slowness. A whispered incantation slipped from her lips as she scattered the sweets into the water, just as the pilot eased the boat away from the dock.

The speedboat tore through the water, leaving the Warri waterfront to fade into a smudge of color behind them. The roar of the engine filled the air, its vibrations syncing with the rhythmic pulse of the river. As the boat veered westward, the chaotic sprawl of ships and tugboats melted into the background, replaced by the eerie stillness of the mangrove swamps.

Here, the river narrowed, and the landscape shifted into something more primal, more menacing. Stout roots jutted out from the water like the legs of ancient, skeletal creatures, tangled in a twisted dance of survival. They clawed their way through the murky depths, rising above the surface as if to capture any unwary traveler who dared enter their domain. The roots formed a grotesque network, a natural labyrinth that seemed to shift and pulse with the flow of the river, their sinewy forms casting twisted shadows across the water. This aspect made Eyouror marvel at nature's mix.

Above, the mangrove trees loomed, their canopies thick with age and mystery. The light struggled to penetrate, filtering through in scattered patches that did little to dispel the growing gloom. The forest here was see-through, but not in the way one might expect; it was as though the air itself had turned to a misty glass, reflecting the dark secrets hidden within the tangled roots and the stirring water below.

At the shoreline, a splash of movement caught Eyouror's attention—tadpoles darting through the shallows, their tiny bodies flickering like shadows among the reeds. Periwinkles clung to the roots and the muddy shore, their spiral shells glinting faintly as the waves from the speedboat lapped against them, the water gently caressing them before growing more insistent, as if trying to coax them from their hold.

The canal twisted and turned, drawing them deeper into a realm of shadows and secrets. The mangrove roots stretched out, reaching for the boat as it passed, their tips grazing the water's surface in a slow, deliberate motion. The speedboat's wake left ripples that disturbed the delicate balance of the shoreline. Tadpoles scattered, the water rippling with their sudden flight, while the periwinkles remained steadfast in their ancient silence.

As the boat pushed forward, the mangroves closed in, their roots a tangle of tripods in this unsettling forest, a silent reminder of the untamed forces lurking beneath the surface. The air grew thick with tension as they ventured further into the unknown, the shadows lengthening with each passing moment.

Eyouror sat in silence taking in all this, her thoughts cloaked in the heavy atmosphere. She tossed biscuits and sweets into the water at intervals, each offering met with a murmured prayer. The boat cut through the water with relentless speed, the sound of its engine a low, persistent growl.

Bennet Island appeared on the horizon, a small outpost on the way to Escravos. Eyouror's eyes swept over the bustling port, the throngs of sailors and traders barely registering as she focused inward, attuning herself to the energies around her. The voice of the sea reached out to her, faint but unmistakable. "Fare thee well, daughter of the realm."

Eyouror's breath caught, her gaze snapping to the water as if seeking the source of the voice. "What's that sound?" she whispered, half to herself, before realizing it wasn't meant for the others. She closed her eyes, drawing in a deep breath. "Oh, be gracious unto me," she murmured, her voice almost lost to the wind.

She forced herself to look deeper into the murky depths below, seeking answers, but only felt the mocking echo of the river's secrets, a soundless laugh that made her shift uneasily on her seat. Her escorts noticed her discomfort but remained silent, their eyes trained on the horizon, wary of disturbing her.

"How long before we reach Escravos?" Eyouror asked, breaking the silence, her voice laced with a tension that matched the churning water beneath them.

The petite man squinted at the horizon. "Just a few more nautical miles," he said, as the boat surged forward. "We're almost there."

Eyouror nodded. "That's fine.'"

The speedboat cut through the choppy waters, spraying mist that clung to Eyouror's skin like a cold whisper. As they neared Escravos, the vastness of the ocean seemed to swallow them whole. The horizon was an endless expanse of gray, merging sky and sea into a single, brooding entity. Eyouror felt a chill creep up her spine, one that had little to do with the damp air.

When they docked, the escorts disembarked first, their movements practiced and efficient. Eyouror followed, her legs unsteady as she stepped onto the slick surface of the dock. The sight of the helicopter waiting for them brought a flicker of something unidentifiable to her eyes, but she masked it quickly, setting her jaw tight as they approached.

The helicopter's rotors began to churn as soon as they were all aboard, the powerful blades slicing through the heavy air. Eyouror's knuckles turned white as she gripped the edge of her seat, her heart racing in time with the rising engine whine. The ground fell away beneath them, and for a moment, she couldn't breathe. She felt giddy being her first experience in an aircraft. Her mind wandered back to the river's depths, to that silent, mocking laugh that had haunted her throughout the boat ride.

The journey to the Royal ship felt interminable. The helicopter's shuddering flight added a new layer to the unease building within her. Below, the ocean was a dark void, its surface roiling with waves that seemed to reach out to pull her down. She forced herself to look away, her eyes settling on the escorts seated opposite her. They were stone-faced, their focus trained outward, but Eyouror caught the furtive glances they exchanged when they thought she wasn't looking.

When the Royal ship finally came into view, looming like a fortress in the middle of the sea, she felt no relief—only a deepening of the tension that coiled tight in her chest. The ship's silhouette was imposing against the bleak sky, its sheer size making her feel small and vulnerable. As the helicopter descended toward the deck, Eyouror swallowed hard, her stomach lurching with the drop.

The moment the skids touched down, she was on her feet, eager to be free of the confined space. The escorts moved with a calm urgency, helping her alight. The deck of the Royal felt solid beneath her feet, but the stability did little to settle her nerves. The wind whipped her hair around her face as she looked up at the towering structure before her.

Eyouror's gaze traveled across the ship, taking in the labyrinth of steel and shadow. The air here was thick with the scent of salt and metal, mingling with something else—something that made her skin prickle with unease. She could sense the eyes of the crew on her, though they were careful to keep their distance, their respect—or fear—evident in every measured movement.

But it was the sea that drew her attention back. The waves crashed against the ship's hull, a relentless reminder of the power lurking just beneath the surface. Eyouror's breath hitched, a memory flashing through her mind—the river's mocking depths, the silent laughter. It was all connected, she knew, but how?

She forced herself to stand tall, her hands clenched at her sides. She couldn't afford to show weakness, not here, not now. The Royal was more than just a ship; it had a football pitch and every luxury thinkable; one could miss one's way if not a guided tour; it was a test, a challenge she had to face head-on. But as she took her first steps forward, a single thought gnawed at the back of her mind: what had she truly signed up for?

~ ~ ~

"Take me to the bow," Eyouror commanded after the initial formalities.

The captain, a tall, handsome Irish man in his forties, with a nod, turned and began a deliberate march along the deck. "Tell the crew to bring the supplies," he ordered the assistant captain by his side without breaking stride.

Eyouror followed, her escorts close behind. The bow loomed ahead, the ship anchored to nothing in particular, but waiting. Waves brushed the hull, the bow lifting and falling in rhythm, the ship seemingly holding its breath. The captain stopped, letting the sea breeze speak for him.

Eyouror leaned over the bow, her fingers curling around the cold metal rail. The ship's hull stood still, pressed against the looming iceberg. The rest of the sea surged around them, waves heaving and crashing against the frozen mass, yet the hull's freeboard clung to it as if tethered by an invisible force.

Her gaze sharpened, tracing the line where the hull's steel met ice. It wasn't the iceberg holding them; the ship should've been nudged back, tossed by the relentless swell. But there it stayed, unmoving, anchored by something unseen, something that defied the chaos around them.

A chill, colder than the northern winds, crept up her spine.

The supplies arrived. Eyouror moved without hesitation, her hands swift and precise. The captain and his crew watched with keen interest as she ripped open the cartons of biscuits and sweets. One by one, she hurled them into the sea at the starboard side of the Royal, then crossed to the port and repeated the act. Sardines followed, sinking beneath the waves as she muttered under her breath.

When she grasped the bottle of Seaman's dry gin, the sea responded, its waves surging violently against the hull. Eyouror's lips curled into a knowing smile. She uncapped the bottle and tipped it, the liquid splashing overboard as she poured the libation. The answer she sought was close, and the ocean roared in anticipation.

Eyouror's hand held steady as the gin cascaded into the sea. The cold air thickened, a hush falling over the crew. A deep, resonant crack echoed across the water, shattering the silence. The icebergs, towering and unyielding, trembled as if something ancient had been disturbed.

Without warning, the ice split, jagged fractures racing across the surface like lightning. The massive structures, once solid, began to crumble. Chunks of ice plummeted into the ocean, sending sprays of icy water high into the air. The Royal shuddered, its metals groaning under the sudden shift.

Eyouror's gaze remained fixed on the disintegrating ice. She continued the libation, the gin flowing freely as the sea devoured the remnants of the once-mighty icebergs. The ship quaked, the crew scrambling to maintain balance. Tension crackled in the air, the ocean's roar growing louder, more insistent.

The icebergs crumbled, leaving only scattered debris in their wake. The Royal glided forward, released at last from the icy prison's grip as the captain signaled his co-pilot to test-run its sail.

Eyouror's eyes sharpened, her true mission now at hand. The crew, watching her command over the sea from the main deck, felt a thrill ripple through their monotony—freedom from the dull days of endless anchorage.

Eyouror's eyes flared with an otherworldly energy as she commanded, "Bring the iron cage."

The captain barked orders, his voice sharp against the wind. Within moments, a six-foot, see-through iron cage large enough for six persons and the supplies clanged onto the ship's bow, its metal glinting in the dull light. Eyouror's gaze swept over it, every inch scrutinized. Satisfied, she gave a curt nod.

"You will lower this cage into the sea," she declared, her tone leaving no room for argument. "And the remaining supplies come with me."

The captain's brow furrowed as he stared at her. "Priestess, this isn't a river; it's the open sea. We can't allow it—it's too risky without proper security measures. You'd need scuba gear to go down there, and the water's freezing."

Eyouror's eyes narrowed, a spark of anger flashing in them. "Then why did you bring me here if you questioned my abilities?"

The captain's face softened, and he lowered his gaze. "I apologize, Priestess. No disrespect intended. I'm just concerned for your safety."

Eyouror's voice held steady, a quiet edge cutting through the tension. "I'll be fine." She reached for the bottle of Seaman's dry gin, her fingers curling around it with a purpose, and stepped into the iron cage. "Give me the keys, and the rest of the supplies."

The captain hesitated, a flicker of dread flashing across his eyes. His hand trembled as he surrendered the keys, the weight of what they signified pressing down on him. He passed her the supplies, each item exchanged with the heaviness of unspoken fears.

"Lower the cage," Eyouror commanded, her tone calm yet unyielding, a finality in her words.

The crew moved with deliberate precision, aligning the crane with the bow. The hook clanked against the cage's upper bar, the sound reverberating through the tense air. Eyouror, undeterred, began her incantations, each word a thread woven into the fabric of the unknown:

no matter how the drafts jostle for space on a river,
the waters never bow, never hold a hyacinth captive.
the sea, a mother, opens her arms to all who seek her embrace.

i call as a daughter of the deep, a plea on my lips,
the sweet rise and fall of my bosom—a lover's toast,
once lost to the world's deceitful dance,
now returned to the waltz of gods and queens.

the seafarer, a mere stranger to the ancient ways,
where quarrels are sealed over wine and honeyed sweets.
eyouror, the one whose gait outshines a king's,
whose heartstrings play to the breast of he who rules,
the swirling depths of the mighty realm of realms.
come, Great One, to this feast of love and mercy...

The cage groaned as the chains tightened, its iron bars gleaming with a cold, unforgiving light. The crew's faces twisted with a mix of fear and grim resolve as they worked, hands trembling despite their training. Eyouror stood motionless inside the cage, her eyes locked on the surface . She could feel the weight of the ocean's secrets pressing against her chest, her pulse quickening with each breath.

The crane lurched, and the cage dipped, the water below churning as if in anticipation. Eyouror's lips moved in silent prayer, her words swallowed by the wind that whipped around her. The sea, once calm, began to stir—ripples spreading outward like whispered warnings.

With a sudden jerk, the cage was airborne, suspended between sky and sea. The crew froze, their eyes darting from Eyouror to the dark waves beneath them. Sweat beaded on their foreheads, the scent of salt and fear thick in the air. The cage swung slightly, casting long shadows across the deck, before the crane arm began its slow, steady descent once more.

Eyouror's heartbeat pounded in her ears as the cage neared the water's surface. The incantations echoed in her mind, a steady rhythm that matched the pulse of the ocean itself. The first touch of seawater was icy, crawling up her bare legs and the iron bars, sending a shiver down her spine. She closed her eyes, focusing on the feel of the cool water against her skin, the sensation grounding her as the cage slipped deeper into the sea.

The crew watched in silence, their fear now a palpable presence, thickening the air with every inch the cage descended. One of them, a young sailor with wide eyes, unconsciously stepped back, his foot catching on a coil of rope. The thud as he hit the deck broke the spell, and all eyes snapped off the cage, now half-submerged.

Eyouror's breath hitched as the cold water climbed to her waist, but surprisingly her white wrapper was not wet. She grinned and tightened her grip on the bars, the once-solid ground of the deck now a distant memory. The cage tilted slightly as it descended further, the water lapping at her shoulders, then her neck. Her heart pounded harder, but she remained still, her gaze fixed on the dark depths below.

The cage plunged deeper into the depths, and for a moment, there was only silence. The crew leaned over the railings, peering into the abyss, their faces pale in the sunlight. Bubbles rose to the surface, a final trace of Eyouror's presence, before the sea swallowed her whole.

Beneath the waves, Eyouror opened her eyes to a rare luminescence near her. The cage swayed gently, the pull of the ocean currents a soft lullaby in her ears. Her heart still raced, but a calmness settled over her, as if the sea itself had accepted her plea. She took a deep breath, her lungs burning with the effort, and began her final solemn prayer, as the depths embraced her. Though the entire cage was submerged and wet, her body remained dry. She had expected this from the onset. The energy closing in on the submerged cage was a clear signal of this.

Above, the crew waited, the minutes stretching into eternity. The sea was calm once more, its surface a mirror reflecting the anxious faces of those who remained on the Royal ship's deck.

~ ~ ~

Eyouror first saw the energy surging towards the cage from the depths, a sudden flash like an arrow loosed from a bow. It spiraled upward, intensifying as it merged with the color of the seawater. The energy took shape, forming a hydra with human features—three heads, two legs, and two hands. Each head moved in perfect harmony with the lower body, its eyes cutting through the seawater and scrutinizing the intruder in the cage.

Eyouror maintained her composure as the creature's growl reverberated around the cage, a low rumble of discontent aimed at the human intruder. "I come in peace," she said, her voice steady despite the tension. "Here's your favorite drink, king of the realm." With a deliberate motion, she opened the cage door and extended the bottle of gin towards him.

The creature's eyes, sharp and penetrating, fixed on the gin. He reached out with a deliberate, calculated movement, grasping the bottle as if it were a prized trophy. He examined it with an intense scrutiny, his expression both inscrutable and expectant.

"Have a sip, great one!" Eyouror urged, her tone laced with both encouragement and underlying tension. "It's your favorite."

The creature paused, eyeing the bottle with a mix of suspicion and curiosity. Then, with a swift motion, he uncorked and tilted it toward his middle head. The liquid flowed eagerly down his throat, its warmth spreading through him.

"Tastes good!" he roared, his voice echoing through the sea as he guzzled more of the gin. The cage crackled with the charged atmosphere, the creature's sudden approval heightening the suspense of the moment.

Emboldened by the creature's eager drinking, Eyouror seized the moment. "Step into this space with me, king of the realm. There's plenty more where this came from." She held up the remaining bottles of gin, her eyes glinting with mischief, and gestured toward the cartons of sardines. The biscuits, already adrift inside the cage.

At that moment, the hydra-headed creature stepped into the cage, the gin clutched in his hand.

Eyouror cleared a space in the cage and gently took his left hand in a gesture of intimacy. His expression softened as he savored the last drop of gin and reached eagerly for the second bottle she held out.

She observed as he downed the second bottle of gin, his movements growing unsteady. With practiced ease, she coaxed him, her voice a smooth caress amid the soothing waves. Noticing his three heads searching for a resting place, she drew him close, offering the warmth of her chest. He nestled against her, surrendering to the comfort of her embrace, and soon drifted into sleep, lulled by the gentle strokes of her fingers.

Eyouror's right hand reached for the stout chain at the top of the cage. She gripped it and yanked with a strength she hadn't known she had, her heart pounding as she waited with bated breath for the outcome. Her fate rested on that single, decisive action.

Moments later, the cage began its ascent, Eyouror's heart soared with elation. The initial sensation of weightlessness soon gave way to a firm, reassuring pull. A wide smile spread across her face, a mix of relief and triumph flooding her senses. The cage continued to rise, and when the crew finally spotted her emergence from the sea's depths, their roar of joy echoed through the air, a thunderous confirmation of their shared victory.

However, they saw she wasn't alone in the cage. A•three-headed, human-like hydra lay nestled in her embrace, its monstrous heads resting against her as if in a deep stupor, unaware of the chaos unfolding around it.

As the cage door creaked open onboard the Royal, Eyouror stepped out, her wrapper and blouse miraculously untouched by the ordeal. The crew's eyes widened at the sight, but she wasted no time.

"Chain him quickly, before he wakes," she commanded, her voice sharp and urgent. "If he stirs now, his wrath will seal our doom." The crew hesitated, glancing at the slumbering hydra, its heads still resting in the cage.

"He is the cause of the icebergs," Eyouror continued, her tone heavy with the weight of what she had uncovered. "It wasn't nature. My task is finished." Her words hung in the air, thick with the finality of her declaration.

The Sign

As THE OLD DUGOUT canoe glided downstream on the sluggish currents, Tamaraukro Opukiri surveyed the swirling drafts of hyacinths on the murky river. In the distance, etched into the edge of a sheer rain forest, the outline of the small village on the promontory weaved a symphony of colors with its rust and newness blending into the complex detail of the dense trees, as if overwhelmed by the magical significance of their shades.

This ensemble of peasants in Ogodobri, known for its relentless notoriety as the hub of militants in the oil rich Riagena, had never slipped from being the foreground of the mystical air of a region in constant flux: the safeguarding of its people from the blatant rape of both the elite and the hawkish corporations rendering it impoverished.

Ironically, they do not know the power at their disposal which can turn the scale of things in their favor, Opukiri thought, wondering how far gone out of tune with their true selves the people had become in the gale of modernity. In a historical sense, the worst sets of people on earth are those ignorant of their spiritual identity...especially when presented with alien gods that threaten their essence of being.

And I am the means through which their truths would be distilled back in whole.

When the canoe eased past a particular spot in the middle of the river where concentric circles stirred the most, Opukiri felt his face tingle with a rush of cold wind rising from the depths, causing goosebumps all over his body. His grip on the wooden paddle tightened with a surge of adrenaline. With his wizened mind in sudden flight, his eyes searched the surface of the river fixedly for clues. The next moment, a warmer gush of air banished the iciness of the prior spot.

Could this be a sign?

The restless writhing of a tilapia amid assorted fish in the bowel of the canoe sent splashes of slimy water on Opukiri's midsection, wetting his stain-ridden fishing robe. He scowled at the fish's unrelenting strive to escape and then shrugged, paddling his canoe towards home aided by a wave of the rainy season's moistened air and the murky river's undulating motions under the pale sun.

The landing of his *egede* on the Ogodobri waterfront rose like a bullhorn before him as he brought the canoe to a stop at the anchor point moments later. Behind it, a compact row of mud cum modern houses on the headland, belonging to his kith and kin he had spent over twenty seasons trying to redirect on spiritual paths, loomed in the light blue sky.

Tamaraukro Opukiri lifted his medium size body from the canoe's stern, his swiftness belied his fifty-five seasons of existence. Placing his paddle on the wet sand near the wooden pole where he tethered the canoe, he stretched his body upwards and sideways like a bowstring to ease tension and then, stooped to fetch the catch for the day – all manner of fish from the canoe into a large white enamel basin by a huge fishing net at the canoe's prow.

As he made to heft the basin onto his head, the bathing spree of a *Lakparada*, a small bird with poker dot plumes, at the fringe of the river, caught his attention. He flinched.

A Lakparada never bathes in broad daylight. Something isn't right, he thought, his eyes shifty with apprehension. A flash memory of the cold spot on the river crossed his mind.

"Give your command, revered Benikrukru," Opukiri pleaded in a hushed tone, "your servant is all ears."

As if in response to his words, Opukiri noticed the *Lakparada* step daintily into the river one more time, dipping his head and half of his body into the subtle waves washing ashore. It then retreated with gusto upland, cleansing itself of the impurities in the river's murk, flapping its wet wings so masterly in a manner likened to a well-orchestrated dance. Once it had rid its wings of the wetness, the *Lakparada* gave a trill and flew across the river to the other bank, tweeting as it went.

Tamaraukro Opukiri's stunned gaze trailed the bird's stylish flight till it merged with the distant horizon as an indescribable speck. Then his mind reeled back to the moment, heart throbbing fast.

Second sign of the day. What gives?

His lips knit into a pout and straightened out in a forced grin, confused about his observation. He hefted the basin of fish onto his head, held the wooden paddle and a cutlass with his right hand, turned towards the rung of steps dug into the mud-baked gradient of the waterfront and clambered up to the row of settlements.

Opukiri moved briskly up the incline, eyes sweeping across his kinsmen and women idling away on the *etele* of the *egede*, exchanging pleasantries with a few of them. Seventy-six degrees out and less fiercer than the flare of a hearth, but the winding paths on his way home were still without the usual bustling of villagers in the mid-morning. Fishermen and women, palm wine tappers, lumber men from the other side of the river, and frolicking children around the houses: all moving through the village like it was the end of their leash of life, anxious daily over trifles.

I've probably missed some hints in the signs of the day, Opukiri thought, *except for the Lakparada's bathing earlier.*

So what does it mean?

Several conflicting thoughts rolled right through Opukiri. The one that survived the night was not only heady but waning. The one that tormented him the most still kept at its torment. The constant echo of Reason seemed to rebound with beaten if not lame excuses for failing to reckon with Benikrukru's pointers. And another array of voices, increasing the weights of the conflicts in his head, demanding their share of attention.

In their separate speeds and directions, his thoughts had no destinations of their own, except this unease which ate at his soul as he walked. He crossed the first threshold to his house, took the sharp bend on the left, saw nothing out of the ordinary, dropped the basin of fish and paddle in a thud on the verandah of his block house, then decided to rest awhile on a wooden bench in front of the house before going back to the waterfront to fetch his fishing net in his canoe. *Maybe I'm just being paranoid over nothing*, he thought. *Or something isn't right.*

What could that be?

Sweat glistened in the waxy dark hair around his temples, cascading to wet his back and sides in rivulets. The sight of a brownish millipede crawling near the slippers on his feet jolted his racing mind back to the present.

What now, Benikrukru?

At that moment, he saw her coming towards him with both hands on her head, wailing.

~ ~ ~

Where could you have gone to, Ediseimi?

Peremene Tamaraukro, almost running, tears streaming down the cleft of her eyes, hair disheveled, wrapper loosely tied around a curvy waist. No major sign of bodily harm: no machete cuts, no gun wounds, no one by her side, no one in chase. Just the uneven breath and the heaving of her chest, as the tears streamed down, blurting her pretty face.

Ediseimi, I know you're alive...

Peremene Tamaraukro, squinting against the sun's fierce rays now, looking beyond the shades cast by the different houses that lined the narrow alley. Teenagers, gawking at her in their innocent stares as she breezed past them ranting about what they could not understand, gave way so as not to be trampled in her hasty strides. Neighbors, peering out through open windows and doorways. Filtering murmurs from concerned kinsmen. The occasional hints of valued loss.

Peremene Tamaraukro. Daughter of Benikrukru's chief priest. Trapped in the warp of a higher power play. Crying. Over loss of a precious diamond. Her only daughter. Seven-seasons-old. Panting, she approached her father's house, a few paces away. Her watery eyes took in the man hunched over a wooden bench. A sigh of relief. He may have the answers to her quest after all.

Father, my oyster is nowhere to be found . . .

~ ~ ~

Upfront, to his left, the thud of a woman's hurried steps. Tamaraukro Opukiri raised his head and winched on the wooden bench; there was no doubt in his mind that he knew the face. There was also no little doubt as to whose face it was. "What now?" he muttered, alarmed by her sad countenance and the shafts of her hair flying in all directions.

An impulsive response. Less than a couple of paces to his spot, she halted, swaying her head back and forth like an unhinged window swinging free: an attractive young woman, with long, braided dark hair and exquisitely chiseled features, looking more disoriented and troubled than in the normal run of things.

Peremene Tamaraukro wiped her tears, eyes flicking upward as if in prayer to the heavens. "Lord, have mercy," she cried, taking a moment to calm her nerves as she reckoned with her father. Then walked up to him, and literally slumped beside him on the bench.

Tamaraukro Opukiri reached out promptly and held her before she hit the bench. Her body quaked against his, and her teeth gritted. Steadying her, Opukiri asked, "What ails you, my child? Why are you so distraught?"

PART TWO

DISTANT HORIZON

ZYLA AND THE VRAL

ZYLA MOVED CLOSER TO the golden throne, his tall frame dwarfed by the immense grandeur of the palace. The gleam of the Wise One's seat reflected in his wide, blue eyes as he glanced at the Vral, seeking answers.

The Vral's lips curled into a knowing smile reckoning with the gangling lad, his amusement palpable. "Son," he said, his voice echoing in Zyla's mind, "you're restless. Perhaps it's time for a bit of adventure."

Zyla's head bobbed in agreement. "Yes," he whispered, the word barely escaping his lips.

"Then sit beside me," the Vral commanded in a gentle tone. "A life-changing journey awaits you, little god of Lemuria."

With hesitant steps, Zyla obeyed, lowering himself onto the seat next to the throne. His gaze sharpened, suspicion flickering in his eyes. "Vral, did you say... little god of Lemuria?"

Vral's eyes darkened with mystery. "We are all gods, Zyla. Capable of more than you can imagine."

"What are we capable of?" Zyla asked, his curiosity sharpening into a mix of wonder and fear.

"You'll find out soon enough."

Zyla noticed the Vral's eyes, dark and enigmatic, scanning the courtyard with a strange intensity. The Vral's immense presence, his towering height, and the dazzling robe that draped his frame, made him appear almost otherworldly to the young boy. Zyla had always thought his father the Vral to be extraordinary, but today, something felt different—mysterious.

"Summon the stone-wings," the Vral ordered, his voice carrying across the palace as his chief counselor bowed and hurried off.

Zyla's thoughts churned with unease. "What is our purpose?" he projected his question into the Vral's mind. "Why are we so blessed? Surely, it must be for something."

The Vral's gaze fixed on Zyla, his expression unreadable. "Nothing is without reason," he finally said, his tone heavy with meaning. "We are not mere chance."

"What does that mean?"

"We are not a cosmic accident," the Vral clarified, his voice hardening. "We have a purpose."

"So, what is it?"

"Come," the Vral said, rising from the throne with surprising swiftness. "It's time to find out, little god of Lemuria."

Zyla's heart pounded in his chest, a mix of fear and excitement as he followed the Vral through the winding corridors of the palace. The courtiers trailed behind, but the Vral's sharp command sent them scattering. "Zyla and I must be alone."

As they emerged into the open courtyard, the Vral's gaze fell upon the stone-wings, now berthed at the entrance of the palace. The sight of it—massive and imposing—sent a shiver down Zyla's spine.

"It is ready, Wise One," the chief counselor reported, his voice trembling with reverence.

"Good," the Vral replied, his tone clipped. "We leave at once."

Zyla's breath caught in his throat as he stared at the stone-wings, a giant boulder with strange markings and a cold, lifeless surface. Yet something about it felt... alive.

With a wave of his hand, the Vral conjured steps that appeared at the boulder's side. He ascended without hesitation. "Come, Zyla," he called over his shoulder, his voice filled with a sense of urgency. "This is the magic of our age."

"What's it for?" Zyla asked, his voice quivering as he climbed the steps after the Vral. Once atop the boulder, he hesitated, casting a fearful glance down. "What now?"

"Patience," the Vral's voice was stern, almost warning. "Patience."

A low hum began to emanate from the stone-wings, growing louder and more intense until, with a sudden jolt, the massive boulder lifted off the ground. Zyla's heart lurched as the stone-wings took flight, its sides expanding into wings of shimmering stone.

"Woohoo!" Zyla gasped, clutching the edge. His voice trembled with a mixture of awe and terror. "This is... terrifying!"

The Vral's gaze flicked sideways to Zyla, his expression indiscernible. "Hold on tight," he murmured.

A sudden gust of wind swept across their faces, and the stone-wings beneath them surged higher, slicing through the air with effortless grace. The horizon expanded, revealing the vastness of the world below, a breathtaking panorama of land and sky melding into one.

Zyla's voice wavered in the rush of the wind. "How do you control this thing?"

"The mind, Zyla. Everything yields to the mind's command." The Vral's voice was calm, but it carried an undercurrent of ancient wisdom, a tone that both reassured and mystified.

"But how?" Zyla's brow furrowed, the words of his father elusive, like the wind itself.

The stone-wings soared on, their robes flapping in the gentle current. The world seemed to hold its breath, watching them.

"The stone-wings are extensions of light," the Vral explained, his voice soft, as if sharing a secret with the universe. "And what greater light is there than the essence of man?"

Zyla shook his head, frustration creeping into his voice. "Light, gods, Lemuria—too many concepts at once, Vral."

The Vral laughed, a sound that echoed through the sky like a sharp breeze. "This flight is more than a lesson, Zyla. It's an awakening. Feel the power that courses through you—a Titan's power."

Zyla's eyes were drawn to the horizon. He saw other stone-wings dotting the sky, gliding like a flock of ethereal birds. He pointed, his voice tinged with excitement. "Look, Vral! More stone-wings!"

The Vral glanced in the direction Zyla pointed but didn't share his excitement. "They aren't real in the way you think. We conjure them when needed, nothing more."

Zyla's joy waned, confusion taking its place. "You're losing me, Vral."

A smile touched Vral's lips, a blend of patience and amusement. "We shape our reality, Zyla. As we choose, so it becomes." He leaned back on the stone-wings, gazing down at the fields and sprawling landscapes below.

"Tell me more," Zyla urged, the mystery only deepening.

"Soon," the Vral promised, but his tone suggested there was much Zyla was not yet ready to grasp.

As if in response to a silent command, the stone-wings veered sharply. The Vral swept his hand through the air, and the mist that had been concealing their path parted like a curtain, revealing a world beyond. Massive beings, their forms towering and majestic, moved about their daily lives.

"These are the Titans," the Vral said, his voice tinged with reverence. "Ancient beings who once roamed these lands. They were genies, Guardians cloaked in human consciousness."

"The Guardians?" Zyla echoed, curiosity sparked.

The Vral's eyes gleamed. "Yes, Guardians. Beings of light, like us. You, Zyla, are one of them—a Guardian."

Zyla's breath caught. "I'm a Guardian?"

The Vral nodded. "We all are."

"But what do we do as Guardians?"

The Vral's grin widened, a knowing look in his eyes. "We protect, guide, and nurture. Each of us is assigned a different aspect of life to watch over. Like the gods in human form we encountered earlier."

Zyla considered this, his mind racing. "And that's all?"

"There's much more," the Vral said, his tone growing solemn. "We're here to express the gift of life, to reconnect with the Light, and ultimately, find our way back to the Source."

Zyla nodded, but the gesture was more one of bewilderment than understanding.

The stone-wings descended slowly, landing in a vast field where giants—beings unlike any Zyla had ever seen—gathered in throngs. Zyla was struck by a strange sensation, as if he could hear their thoughts, feel their emotions, like echoes in his heart.

"I can hear them," Zyla whispered, wonder filling his voice. "Their thoughts... they unfold before me like a story, like a flower opening its petals."

The Vral smiled. "This is part of your journey, Zyla. We don't need words to communicate—thoughts are enough. And travel, it's not bound by the physical. Now you see why I say we're gods?"

The Vral stretched out his hand, and a large blackbird swooped down, landing gracefully on his palm. "Go, tell the clan—the Vral is coming," he said to the bird, which cawed and flew off with a sense of purpose.

Zyla stared in awe. "You talk to birds too?"

The Vral chuckled. "We're connected to all living things, Zyla. They're as much a part of the Light as we are. You just need to tune into their frequency."

Stepping off the stone-wings, the Vral walked with a casual grace across the dewy grass, his steps deliberate, as if he were in no rush. He gestured for Zyla to follow, and they moved together towards a distant community.

At the edge of the field, the Vral paused and touched a single blade of grass, his fingers brushing its sharp edge. He closed his eyes, his thoughts directed inward. "What is your purpose?" he asked silently.

Zyla watched, puzzled by what seemed like an odd ritual. But then, a voice—a faint whisper—resonated in both their minds. "I am a healer," the grass said. "Use me to cure ailments."

Zyla's eyes widened as the words seeped into his consciousness. "Plants... talk?"

The Vral ignored Zyla's astonishment, his focus entirely on the grass. "What kind of ailment?" he asked.

"The kind that afflicts the heart," came the soft reply.

Zyla couldn't contain his surprise. "Medicine for the heart?"

"Shhh," the Vral cautioned, bringing a finger to his lips. His attention returned to the grass. "How do we use you?"

"My essence is all you need," the grass responded.

The Vral nodded thoughtfully. "Is that all?"

The grass's laughter was like the rustling of leaves in a breeze. "The gods always want more. But I'll tell you a secret—I am magic."

"How so?"

"Speak to me with intention, and your desires will manifest."

The Vral's eyes lit up with curiosity. He carefully plucked the blade of grass, placing it gently in his palm.

"Ouch! That stings!" the grass protested, squirming slightly.

"My apologies," the Vral said with a soft smile. "I didn't mean to harm you. I'm eager to test your power."

"Go ahead," the grass sighed.

The Vral closed his eyes and made a wish. "Take us to the beginning of all things."

"That's a grand request," the grass murmured, "but it can be done. Hold your son's hand."

The Vral obeyed without hesitation.

"Repeat these words after me," instructed the grass, its voice a whisper through the rustling blades. "I am an energy form, free and boundless, pulsing through creation. Let my essence unfold as it did in the beginning, for I desire unity of purpose."

The Vral's feet tingled as he intoned the words, "I am an energy form, free and boundless, pulsing through creation. Let my essence unfold as it did in the beginning, for I desire unity of purpose."

As the final syllable left his lips, a shiver coursed through Zyla and the Wise One. The air around them thickened with a palpable energy, swirling and lifting the mist from the emerald field. An unseen force wrapped around them, pulling their very souls upward into a yawning portal that split the hazel sky.

They hurtled through the vortex, hands tightly clasped, eyes wide with awe as the cosmos unfurled before them. Stars, galaxies, and the infinite stretch of space seemed to dissolve as they ascended, their ethereal forms shedding like the scales of a serpent, one by one. Each loss of their luminous bodies made them feel lighter, as though they were shedding the burdens of their existence.

With every increment of their ascent, the clamor of Lemuria and its myriad troubles grew fainter, like echoes in a distant cave. They drifted away from their corporeal concerns, becoming increasingly aware of their true essence—a mere condensation of pure Light. The celestial expanse around them revealed new truths. The vast blue sky was more than a canvas for clouds and stars; it was a gateway to the primordial Source, the birthplace of all creation. Their physical forms had vanished, but their consciousness persisted as delicate specks of pure Light.

As they ventured deeper into the unknown, Zyla heard the Wise One's voice cutting through the void. "Man's journey to Lemuria and beyond is but a fleeting speck of Light emerging from the Black Hole. Now, do you perceive the ocean of Light?"

Zyla struggled to grasp the profound words, only to feel a sudden, disorienting shift. In an instant, they found themselves back in the familiar green field of Lemuria, their bodies restored and the ethereal journey seemingly erased from reality. The Vral's enigmatic message hung in the air, as elusive and profound as ever.

FATE

At the threshold of the ancient mountains, Netu Deo felt the atmosphere crackle with a tangible, electric energy. The ground beneath him vibrated with a hum that seemed to writhe from the heart of the planetoid itself. To his right, a deep canyon carved its way through the land, while to his left, the hills rolled like silent sentinels, watching over the mist-filled valley below.

Ahead, the castle loomed, an impossible blend of delicate glass and timeless marble, glowing softly in the warm light. It was as if the structure had grown from the very bones of the planet, its design a mix of old-world grandeur and something far beyond human comprehension. The entire planetoid shimmered with a light that seemed to seep from its core, casting beautiful shadows that danced across the valley.

Netu could feel the weight of the ages like a shroud over his senses, the castle standing as a testament to time's passage and the mysterious forces that had shaped this place. He took a step forward, the sense of something lurking just beyond his understanding pulling him closer to the ancient architecture, each breath tightening the knot of suspense in his chest.

Netu scanned the landscape, his eyes narrowing as he searched for any sign of life. But there was nothing—no birds in the hazel sky, no insects buzzing in the air, not even the rustle of wind through the trees. The planetoid was unnaturally still, a world frozen in time. The quiet was so complete it seemed to press in on him, amplifying every breath, every heartbeat, until the silence became a living thing, wrapping itself around him like a shroud.

His gaze drifted back to the castle, its walls gleaming in the ghostly light. Something was happening inside, something he could feel in the pit of his stomach. The air around him grew heavier as if the very atmosphere was bracing for what was to come. He moved forward, his steps cautious, the sense of impending conflict thickening with every passing second.

Inside the castle, the tranquility outside gave way to a different kind of tension. On the second floor, in the largest room, three men moved with purpose. Their footsteps echoed against the reflective floor, but their voices were silent, their communication done in gestures and glances. The fair-skinned man and the older man with dark skin reached the center of the room first, their eyes fixed on the younger man who trailed behind, momentarily distracted by the shimmering glass walls and the illusionary patterns on the ceiling. A sharp gesture from the older man snapped him back to attention, and he quickly joined them.

Without a word, the three men nodded in agreement, their focus drawn to a point high above. The younger man, his muscles taut with youth and strength, moved first. He bent his knee, offering himself as a ladder for the older man to climb. The older man, moving with the grace of someone who had done this before, hoisted himself onto the younger man's shoulders, his eyes measuring the distance to the ceiling.

But it wasn't enough. He teetered for a moment, his body straining to reach the mosaic tiles above. With a swift adjustment, he steadied himself, then reached down to pull the fair-skinned man up. The three of them now formed a precarious human tower, their bodies stretching toward the ceiling as if defying gravity itself.

Sweat beaded on the fair-skinned man's brow as he reached for the hidden latch in the ceiling. His fingers brushed against the cool surface, searching, probing until they found the small, square tile that concealed the passageway. With a grunt of effort, he pushed the tile aside, revealing a dark opening just wide enough for a man to slip through. He glanced down at the others, his eyes conveying the unspoken question. They responded with a brief nod, urging him on.

He pulled himself up, his body disappearing into the darkness above, leaving the other two men below, their hearts pounding as they waited, their muscles tensed for whatever would come next. The castle seemed to hold its breath, the silence deepening, as if the planetoid itself was aware of the imminent danger lurking just beyond the thin veil of reality.

The younger man tightened his grip around the older man's legs as he let go of the fair-skinned man, who was now safely inside the ceiling. Relief washed over him as the weight on his shoulders lessened, but the urgency of their mission kept his mind sharp. This wasn't just about physical strain—it was about survival. Failure was not an option.

The room fell silent again, the oppressive stillness returning as the older man climbed down from his perch. They exchanged a quick, tense look, their muscles twitching with nervous energy. The eerie calm pressed down on them, the quiet stretching out like a predator waiting to pounce.

For what felt like an eternity, they fidgeted in the silence, the weight of the unknown pressing on them. Then, a faint sound—a scuttling above—broke the stillness. Both men froze, eyes snapping up to the ceiling. What was up there? Their hearts pounded as they waited, each second dragging on.

A few strands of blonde hair appeared first, slipping down through the opening in the ceiling, followed by the face of the fair-skinned man peering down at them. They felt a brief surge of elation, though uncertainty still gnawed at their nerves. The man above withdrew for a moment, then reappeared with a soft call, "Here—" as he carefully lowered a small khaki pack through the opening.

The pack wasn't large, but as it slid through the ceiling, the two men below knew it held something of immense value—perhaps more than just gold or diamonds. No words were needed; they all understood that this sack contained something far more precious—the secret to life itself.

The older man, with a steady hand, caught the sack with a gentle precision. The younger man watched, his eyes wide, taking in the moment without a hint of envy, only the weight of responsibility. Meanwhile, the fair-skinned man hung from the ceiling, his hands gripping the ledge as he prepared to drop. He released himself, landing heavily on the terrazzo-like floor with a dull thud. The two men rushed to his side, but he waved them off, a heroic smile spreading across his face despite the impact.

The older man, his thick beard framing a face etched with determination, turned to the younger man and handed him the sack. "Now go!" he ordered, his voice firm. He pointed towards the door, urgency flashing in his eyes. But the younger man hesitated, confusion flickering across his features. He glanced at the sack, then at the door.

"Go!" the older man barked, his tone leaving no room for doubt. The younger man's hesitation vanished, and he spun around, sprinting toward the door. The weight of the sack seemed to pull him forward, the secret it contained driving him on. The mission was far from over, and as he ran, the ominous sense of impending conflict hung thick in the air, waiting to explode.

In a sudden flash, Netu Deo realized that the younger man—running with the sack clutched to his side—was him. The command to "Go!" echoed in his mind, pushing him forward with no clear direction, only a primal instinct guiding his every step. He burst through the swivel glass door, finding himself on a terrace that led to a stairway on the left. He sprinted up, taking the stairs two at a time, the bannister his only aid, until he emerged onto the eastern summit of the castle.

The rooftop was a flat, expansive landing space, likely designed for space saucers. From here, he had a sweeping view of the mountain range, but no clear escape. The cliffs were steep and unforgiving, with no stairway or path leading down from the castle's high walls. The northern peaks stretched without end, an unscalable fortress of rock. The western perimeter was fortified by tall, intricate marble tapestry, blocking any route of escape. South-west, a cleft in the mountain seemed the only possibility, a dangerous descent into a valley that lay between the mountain and distant hills.

His mind raced, trying to piece together a plan, when suddenly, movement caught his eye. A towering figure charged toward him—an old acquaintance from Earth, now consumed with hostility or envy. Netu Deo's instincts screamed at him to flee, and without hesitation, he bolted, the treasure sack held tightly against his ribs.

He knew where he had to go—the cleft in the mountain was his only hope. But as he sprinted down the stairs and across the terrace, his mind clouded with fear. The man's footsteps echoed behind him, closing in with terrifying speed. There was no time to find a hidden doorway or utter a secret passphrase. He refused to become prey, especially not with the treasure he carried.

He dashed to the right of the terrace, ahead of his pursuer by mere meters. There, a high marble slab lined the stockade. Without thinking, he leaped for it, surprised when his fingers caught the edge despite the sack in his grasp. He hoisted himself up, pain shooting through his muscles, but he was relieved to find a hidden stairway leading down.

Descending quickly, he reached the castle's first segment, then further down to the basement, where a massive electronic steel door awaited. It slid open as he approached, as though anticipating his arrival. Paranoia tugged at him—was he being watched? But there was no time to dwell on that. He burst through the door and onto the mountain, racing toward the gorge.

His descent was frantic, sliding down the cliffside, grasping at jutting rocks to slow his fall. Finally, he tumbled into the gorge's embrace, only slightly bruised. Glancing back, he saw the tall man was still chasing him, gaining ground. The gorge funneled into a valley, but the sight that greeted him was horrifying. The valley floor was a molten swamp, a treacherous landscape that clung to his legs and tripped him. He fell hard, his body sinking into the muck, but the sack remained tightly in his grasp.

He forced himself up, his body screaming in protest, and staggered along the firmer bank of the valley. His breath came in ragged gasps, his vision blurred by pain and exhaustion. Yet, when he glanced back, the towering figure was gone, vanished as if swallowed by the planetoid itself.

The terrain shifted abruptly, and Netu Deo found himself climbing a steep slope, the valley behind him morphing into a mountain that seemed to grow with every step. The narrow path—a mere foot and a half wide—rose sharply, a precarious ascent that led to a crest and continued as a thin, straight line along the mountain's length.

He reached the horizontal ledge, knowing that one wrong move could send him plummeting into the swift river below, where ominous catacombs awaited. He inched forward, his back scraping against the rough mountain wall, his hands searching for purchase. The effort was agonizing, but he pressed on, his mind focused on survival.

Finally, the path veered downward, leading him closer to the river. The ground widened, forming a natural pathway that stopped at the water's edge. A narrow bridge not more than two-planks in berth stretched across the river, leading to a colossal crystal sphere on the other side. The sphere glinted in the distance, a structure so grand it seemed to belong to another world—perhaps even another planetoid.

Netu's heart pounded as he approached the bridge, knowing that whatever lay beyond was as uncertain as the path he had just traversed. But there was no turning back now, only forward, toward the unknown that awaited him on the other side.

The sounds of life from the crystal sphere—humanoids scurrying with glee, bottle-like objects clashing, drums pounding in frenzied rhythm—hinted at a thriving civilization. Netu Deo stood on the brink, the bridge before him a narrow oak plank, the only link across the time-warped divide between the two worlds. The contrast struck him; the planetoid on which he stood felt like a mere transit station, a stepping stone, unlike the lively realm before him.

He watched as one by one, people emerged from his side, each attempting the crossing as if it were some ultimate test. Four had already tried by the time he arrived. Each met the same fate—venturing across the slippery plank only to lose their footing near the middle or close to the other side, plummeting into the roaring river below. The water swallowed them with a finality that chilled him.

Netu Deo knew he would have to cross the bridge too. Failure felt inevitable, yet he had no choice. Then, a thought sparked in his mind, a glimmer of hope. The others had walked straight ahead, trying to maintain balance on the slick surface. It hadn't worked for any of them. The solution struck him—sideways. Just like on the narrow ledge of the mountain, he could glide sideways, keeping his center of gravity low. A grin formed on his face, the first since leaving the castle.

The treasure sack was gone—vanished without a trace. His hands were free as he took the first cautious step onto the plank. He moved quickly, turning sideways and gliding across, one foot sliding in front of the other. The plank creaked under his weight, but he kept his focus straight ahead, refusing to look at the swirling depths below.

The bridge held. Step by step, Netu Deo moved closer to the far side, the crystal globe looming larger with each glide. The roar of the river beneath him faded as he neared the end. A final leap, and he landed safely on the other side, standing at the oval doorway of the gleaming sphere. A rush of triumph surged through him. He had made it—against all odds, he had crossed the time warp.

Inside the crystal sphere, the world was a dazzling spectacle. The planetoid, as he now understood it to be, teemed with life. Gold sparkled underfoot, and diamonds adorned the magnificent structures. The crystal walls allowed a clear view out, while from the outside, they shone with an impervious brilliance, a shield against whatever lay beyond.

The inhabitants were humanoids, the source of the lively sounds he had heard. They feasted with abandon, children laughing, adults engrossed in animated, often vulgar conversations. Giant beings—extraterrestrials—joined in, drumming in sync with the revelry. Their language was an indecipherable mix of sounds, adding to the chaotic atmosphere.

Despite their friendly demeanor, Netu's refusal to partake in their offerings of food and drink didn't go unnoticed. They welcomed him with open arms, yet his aloofness seemed to puzzle them. He wandered from table to table, hoping for some explanation, some purpose for his presence on this strange planetoid.

But all he found was indulgence—a world dedicated to the pleasures of the moment. The feasting, the drinking, the laughter—it all felt hollow.

Disappointment gnawed at him. Was this the end of his journey, the ultimate truth? The people of the globe seemed uninterested in anything beyond their hedonistic pursuits.

He retreated to the doorway, staring out at the distant mountain range he had crossed. The thrill of victory felt empty now, overshadowed by the purposelessness of it all. He contemplated going back, retracing his steps across the bridge. But something held him back. He stood there, watching the undulating peaks, his mind heavy with questions.

Then, without warning, a brilliant web of light engulfed the entire planetoid. The light radiated with an intensity that consumed everything in its path, dissolving the sphere and the world he had just entered. In an instant, the space around him became a void, a timeless chasm where the planetoid had once been.

Netu Deo, caught in a pocket of light particles, hovered above the emptiness. He watched, stunned, as the world beneath him vanished, leaving only a void in its wake. And there, suspended in the infinite silence, he realized he had crossed a threshold far greater than any bridge.

Untold Truths

Netu Deo sat cross-legged, the cool earth beneath him anchoring his lithe frame as his dark brown eyes remained shut, his face set in quiet concentration. His thirty-three-years old body, though still, thrummed with a hardly contained energy, like a wire stretched taut, ready to hum at the faintest vibration. Muscles rippled beneath his skin, not from tension but from the power surging through his veins, energy drawn from something far beyond his mortal flesh. His breath slowed, deepened, and with each exhale, his awareness stretched further, thinning the veil between man and the infinite.

A subtle light danced behind his eyelids—waves of it, soft and pulsing, like echoes of stars long extinguished. It rose from within him, a swirling sea of cosmic force that churned silently in his chest, its rhythm synced to a hum that now vibrated through the air around him. His close-cropped dark hair gleamed under an unseen glow, while the semi-broad line of his nose remained a steady anchor in the storm of sensation.

He felt the sensation intensify, spreading through his limbs, his mind expanding past the edges of thought, dissolving the boundary between self and universe. The question—silent, primal—surfaced: Africa, the birthplace of civilizations. What histories lay buried beneath its wounds? His inquiry rippled outward, blending with the ancient pulse of the Higher Intelligence.

"You have asked; you shall know."

The words echoed, clear as crystal, resonating all around him. Then came the silence. No sound, no breath. Only stillness. And yet, within that stillness, a powerful vibration seized his body, surging through him like wind through a taut string. His being shifted, light as air, as though the weight of flesh no longer bound him. He did not resist. He simply waited, motionless, as time stretched into eternity.

Slowly, the ground of his existence melted away, the edges of his reality blurring into something deeper, older. He felt himself pulled—no, drawn—out of the present moment, not by force but by a gentle, pristine thread. The pull wasn't through mere time but through epochs, until he stood in the midst of ancient Africa, staring at the face of the forgotten Atlantis, the cradle of all. Here, the scars of history glistened with untold truths, ready to unfold before him.

He blinked, his senses flooded with a sudden clarity. Before him stretched a river, its surface gleaming like liquid glass. The current moved with an unsettling slowness, each ripple gliding as if time itself hesitated to disturb the peace. On the far bank, the horizon expanded in endless abundance, a wilderness untouched by human hands. Life thrived, but in strange, ancient forms—yet no human trace disrupted the landscape. The essence of an earth far removed from the one he knew filled the air.

Netu's gaze fell to the shoreline at his feet. A thin layer of golden sand stretched out, glistening under a sun that seemed suspended between warmth and a faint crimson glow. Scattered across the sand lay the remnants of countless mollusks, their shells forming a loose bed of shimmering fragments. The river's sluggish current brushed against them with a lifeless, delicate grace. They sparkled, their beauty unnervingly vibrant for things long dead, the sunlight catching in their iridescent curves like a cruel joke played by nature.

The dead shells seemed to mock life's fleeting nature. Once living creatures, they had now become nothing more than ornaments for the sand, their gleam a silent testimony to the paradox of existence. Why, Netu wondered, was there such beauty in death? What twisted irony gave birth to this spectacle—a show where life's end brought about something more perfect, more serene than its beginning? It was as though the earth celebrated the finality of death, immortalizing these shells in their stillness, their gleam a taunting reminder of the thin line between life and nothingness.

As these thoughts rippled through his mind, a sudden burst disturbed the calm. The water, just a few feet from where he stood, erupted in a violent ripple. His heart lurched. The surface split, not from the gentle undulation of the current, but from something below—a force rising from the depths. Netu's breath caught as he watched, unable to move, unable to tear his gaze from the disturbance.

Then, from the center of the growing ripples, a dark figure broke through the surface. A human form, male, emerging from the river, his skin brown and gleaming under the strange light. Netu's pulse raced, his legs felt unsteady, like they were made of rubber, hardly able to keep him standing. Fear clawed at his chest, yet his eyes remained locked on the figure.

He watched as the man waded toward him, water cascading off his torso, naked from the waist up, his muscular frame rippling with power and intent.

Before Netu could fully process the sight, more movement stirred the water. Three more figures surfaced behind the man, their presence sending another thrill of fear and excitement coursing through his veins. The tallest among them carried two smaller figures, one strapped to his body with what looked like a woven cloth, and the other right in front. They moved with purpose, their dark skin radiating a faint golden glow, a sharp contrast to the cool, stagnant water from which they had risen.

Netu's mind spun, overwhelmed by the eerie beauty, the stillness now disrupted by these mysterious beings. He knew instinctively that this was no ordinary encounter, no ordinary place. Something ancient, something forgotten, was unfolding before him, and as the figures approached, a shiver of recognition crept down his spine.

Netu stood at the water's edge, his eyes following the strange family as they waded toward him with effortless grace. The man, the woman, and two children moved through the river as if the current bent to their will, their strides smooth and practiced. For a moment, his mind wandered, and he almost convinced himself they were merely a family out for a simple joy of nature. But he quickly brushed the thought aside. Where could they have come from? There was no settlement in sight. His view of the horizon stretched far, revealing nothing but the vast, untamed wilderness.

As they drew closer, the water now waist-deep around them, a spark of recognition flared in Netu's chest. His heart thudded. The man's face—where had he seen it before? The lines of his features stirred something deep within Netu, something ancient, buried so far back in his memory that he struggled to grasp it. Time itself seemed to pull him back, dragging his thoughts to the distant past. This man was no stranger; he belonged to a time older than the world Netu knew.

The voice came again, a quiet murmur that seemed to rise from within the earth itself, echoing in his mind.

"This is Africa—Atlantis as it once was."

Netu's gaze sharpened, his focus narrowing on the family now stepping out of the water onto the shore. The fine grains of sand sparkled beneath their feet, shells catching the last glimmers of the day's light. He stood high above them, his vantage point giving him a sense of distance, of safety. They hadn't seen him, or at least, they hadn't acknowledged him. He wasn't sure whether to feel relief or concern.

Then, as if guided by some unseen force, the man broke away from the others. He veered from the path they had been on and began climbing toward Netu's position with steady, deliberate steps. Netu's pulse quickened, but his feet remained rooted. There was something in the man's movements—an unspoken message, a beckoning presence that filled the air with a weight that made it hard to breathe.

As the man reached the small patch of earth where Netu stood, the ground shifted beneath his feet. The soil cracked and groaned, rising upward, lifting the man with it. A great boulder pushed through the earth as though some ancient hand had summoned it, and slowly, it pivoted, its massive weight defying reason. Netu could only watch, stunned, as the man stood atop it, his bare chest gleaming in the dim light, his presence larger than life.

The boulder continued its slow, deliberate turn, until it rested at a slight angle beyond Netu. Without hesitation, the man leapt from its peak, landing gracefully as the rock settled back into the earth. A grin spread across his face, and with an eerie calm, he approached Netu, the woman and children close behind.

Tension coiled in Netu's chest, fear creeping along his spine. He could feel it building, that primal instinct to run, but he remained frozen, his mind racing as they neared him.

Then the man spoke, his voice low but commanding, directing his words to the woman. The language was familiar to Netu, though its meaning was laced with something darker, more profound than mere words.

"Tell the eldest to follow him," the man said, gesturing toward Netu.

The woman obeyed without question, nudging the eldest child forward. The boy, his grin wide and eager, walked toward Netu with a confidence that chilled him. The woman turned away, heading toward a place Netu had not noticed before, his attention too fixed on their emergence from the river.

When he finally turned to look, he saw them—buildings, few but striking, their form reminiscent of structures from a time long past. They rose out of the earth like ghosts, their presence both surreal and undeniable, shrouded in mystery, pulling Netu deeper into the unknown.

Netu stood on the steep edge, the higher community spread out before him like a rare jewel nestled against the river. The buildings, sparse but magnetic in their beauty, blended seamlessly with the wild, untamed vegetation that circled the land. He hadn't quite finished marveling at this strange discovery when the eldest boy beside him grew restless, tugging at his hand. The pull jolted him from his reverie, and he smiled, taking the boy's hand. His eyes drifted toward the man from the river, who stood nearby, watching—present, yet distant. There was something about him, an aura that thrummed quietly in the air.

Then, suddenly, it broke. A sharp scuffling noise cut through the stillness, slicing up from behind them, somewhere inland. Netu stiffened, the sound coming from a hundred meters away. Without a word, the man from the river snapped to attention, his demeanor shifting. He was off, moving quickly up the slope, his strides sure and purposeful. Netu hadn't missed the signs—the way the man carried himself, the way others subtly deferred to him. He was no ordinary man. He was a leader, the crown of authority resting invisibly on his head.

As he strode inland, his speed only increased. The land's gentle incline did little to slow him down, and Netu, still holding the boy's hand, followed at a cautious distance. They approached the outskirts of the community where the argument raged. The voices grew louder as the man neared, though his presence alone should have calmed them. But the quarrel worsened.

Netu stopped, watching from a safe distance as the crown-head made his approach. Just before he reached the heart of the scuffle, a herd of plump cows and sheep lounging by the path caught his attention. He paused—only for a moment—but what Netu saw next sent a ripple of unease through him.

The man spoke to the animals. Not in passing, but with genuine intent, a language that Netu somehow understood, though it wasn't his own. The animals responded, not with mindless bleats, but with a gravity that matched the man's tone. There was a connection between them, a silent, unbreakable bond of mutual respect. It was as though they were equals, the animals recognizing the man's authority, just as the man respected their existence.

Netu's heart quickened. He watched as the man patted two of the creatures gently on the head before continuing his march toward the quarrel. The strange encounter shook something loose in Netu, a whisper of ancient mystery clawing its way back into his consciousness. He stood frozen, trepidation creeping into his chest, watching as the man prepared to confront the discord ahead.

The tension simmered in the air as the man's command silenced the squabbling youths. "Now stop the argument, it is not necessary. Let me give you your own houses." His voice was low, calm—yet it sliced through the commotion with an authority no one dared challenge.

Their faces tightened with suppressed complaints, but Netu could feel their resistance weaken. It was clear that accommodation was the cause of their bickering—a lack of it, perhaps. The crown-head didn't seem to need an explanation, as though he already knew. Some strange link, a connection to their minds, perhaps.

The crown-head began to chant, his voice rising from soft murmurs to something far more forceful. What started as an almost private whisper swelled into an incantation, his words wrapping around the moment with a pulse of power.

And then, as he fixed his eyes on the earth beneath him, it happened.

The ground trembled, a low rumble at first, like the earth groaning in protest. But it wasn't long before the tremor grew into something grave. The land beneath them feet quaked violently, sending them all into an anxious confusion. They exchanged glances, unsure whether to run or stay. Yet the crown-head, with a slight wave of his hand, signaled for them to remain still, to trust in his control. But their nerves frayed as the earth beneath them felt alive, threatening to tear itself apart. A thrill coursed through Netu, the excitement of the unknown clashing with the terror of what might come next.

A crack split open the ground near them, a jagged line racing toward the horizon, cutting deeper as it stretched. The ground beneath them shifted, pulling them further away on a sliver of earth that had once been whole. It was as though the very land was splitting into two worlds, and they were caught between these. The crown-head stood with them on this new landmass, calm, a slight grin playing on his lips. He showed no fear—he had orchestrated this, after all. Netu and the others were the ones panicking, not him.

The earth shook again, but this time, something far deeper stirred. The incantation hadn't ended. The crown-head's eyes were locked on the widening chasm, and from within, something began to rise. Netu edged closer, daring to peer into the abyss.

What emerged was overwhelming. A landmass, square and immense, pushed itself up from the earth's core. Its surface gleamed with a civilization more advanced than any Netu had known—its buildings intricate, a network of roads threading through its expanse. Yet, despite its grandeur, there was something primal in the way the mud houses stood, a testament to a heritage long forgotten but never fully erased.

As it rose, the new landmass seamlessly slid into place, filling the gap left by the rift. It expanded the land, merging the old with the new, doubling the scope of what had once been. The crown-head had restored the earth—no, he had enhanced it. The split was no longer a divide but a bridge between two worlds.

Netu stood, dumbstruck, as did the others. The youths who had argued moments ago now gawked, their complaints forgotten in the awe of what they had witnessed. The crown-head, his incantation complete, turned to them with a satisfied grin. "You can pick your choice of accommodation among the lot," he said, gesturing toward the new world he had summoned.

The tension drained from the crowd, replaced by eager excitement. They rushed forward, eager to claim their share of the new land. Yet, as Netu followed, his curiosity was not about property but the people—these dark-skinned mortals, radiant with the light of an ancient lineage. They moved through the new civilization with ease, embracing both the old ways and the new.

Through the winding paths, he saw their lives unfold—the mud huts beside grander homes, the bare bodies glistening in the sun, the joyous celebrations of a people not overwhelmed but alive with the pulse of their shared history. This was more than a merging of lands; it was a merging of time, of cultures, of stories yet untold.

The boy, the one who had wandered off from the river, darted away from Netu's side, his earlier whimpers dissolving into excitement. Netu didn't try to stop him; the child, like the others, was drawn to the shifting pulse of the new civilization. Around him, people scattered, feet pounding the earth in a chaotic rhythm as they rushed to claim what seemed to be theirs by right—a birthright bestowed by the crown-head. The roadways and footpaths buzzed with frantic energy, as if the land itself had awoken beneath them, urging them forward.

Netu moved swiftly, the energy of the crowd stirring something deeper in him. He joined a lively group of men and women, their laughter sharp in the air, their steps quick as they made for a dense thicket of buildings—bungalows rising from the earth like newly grown trees. But while they hurried to occupy and conquer, Netu sought something else.

His gaze swept over the scene—brown-skinned mortals with an ancient presence moved through the streets, their dark-hued, glistening bodies standing out against the backdrop of mud huts and modest homes. At each corner, he glimpsed pieces of a life untouched by time. There were the half-naked figures, their blackness radiant, engaged in a raw celebration of this newfound world. They drank from gourds, flirted with ease, their naturalness unburdened by the pressures of change.

Yet, beneath this surface, Netu sensed an unspoken tension. These people, so rooted in tradition, did not seem overwhelmed by the alterations in their environment. No, they wore their heritage like armor, unmoved by the looming shadow of progress. Their eyes, bright with intelligence, flickered with awareness—they knew what was coming, but they remained as they were. The air thickened, charged with the quiet threat of conflict, as if the land, the people, and Netu himself were all waiting for something to break.

Netu strode through the narrow passage, his eyes sharp as he navigated the path. A square-headed, obese kid sprang from one of the buildings, weaving and taunting him, blocking his way with exaggerated movements. Netu did not falter. His advance was calm, resolute, as if the boy's antics were nothing but an afterthought. The kid hesitated, realizing his efforts were useless, and stepped aside, his giggling soon joined by the sound of his friends rushing to the verandah nearby.

Three more brats appeared, laughing, their skimpy pants swaying as they pointed at Netu. The sound of their glee echoed, attracting the attention of some elderly men and women. They paused from sipping their gruel, their eyes narrowing, whispers crawling between them. Though their language was foreign, Netu understood the tone well enough. They saw him as an outsider, someone who didn't belong. One wrong move, and they'd confirm him as a threat, a pariah

Netu offered a guarded smile, masking his unease, and moved quickly past them.

Reaching the waterfront, he found the rock-elevator resting where the crown-head had left it. Without the incantations, it was just stone—cold and lifeless. Netu stepped onto the platform, instinct urging him forward. The plan was simple: rise above the village, survey the land, and intimidate the people from a height, like a descending saint rather than an alien. But the rock refused to move.

He closed his eyes, willing it to rise, concentrating until his brow tightened. Nothing. The rock sat still, mocking him with its refusal. Another effort—another failure. Frustration surged, and he cursed himself under his breath, feeling the weight of his inadequacy.

Abandoning the effort, he gazed out over the sprawling civilization below, his eyes tracing the intricate patterns of culture woven into the landscape. The harmony of the place was undeniable—a society so entwined with nature that it seemed more dream than reality. For a moment, Netu marveled at it, awed by the simplicity and strength that coexisted in this ancient land.

Then, the voice returned, clear and unyielding.

"You wanted to see the Africa of old, didn't you?" it asked, gentle yet commanding.

Netu stiffened, his body tensing as the voice wrapped around his thoughts.

"You'd make it easier on yourself if you stripped away that drunkenness," the voice continued, a subtle rebuke.

He blinked, realizing he had been too overwhelmed—whether by excitement or fear, he didn't know. Calming himself, he focused, letting the tension drain away. He could feel the pulse of the land beneath him, watching as it watched him in return.

The voice resumed, warmer now, filling his mind with clarity.

"Welcome to Olden Africa, the first in the line of Atlantis civilizations," it explained, and Netu listened intently, his breath steadying. "You stand on the soil of the first human civilization. The Africa you know is but a shadow of this. Back then, it was a giant globe, undivided by continents. That dismembering came much later—violent shifts, splinters of what once was whole, a testament to the Masters who reshaped power."

The voice paused, letting him absorb the revelation. Netu's mind spun, the weight of history and mystery pressing down on him, but he remained silent, his gaze fixed on the world before him, and the secrets it held.

Netu stood still, eyes narrowing as he tried to process the discord between what he knew and what lay before him. The olden Atlantis—its simplicity felt almost barbaric, a world stripped of the familiar luxuries of the contemporary age. He could almost see it, spinning in a primitive cycle, devoid of the mechanical hustle of cars, trains, and planes. But there was a paradox gnawing at him, a strange tension in knowing that this supposedly "primitive" civilization had reached an ascension far beyond the present age. Outwardly docile, they had achieved psychic heights unimaginable today.

His thoughts twirled in a quiet storm. How could a people so advanced in consciousness rely on no visible technology, no grand infrastructures of transportation? The streets of Old Afrièa bore no trace of engines or steel. He shook his head. Was it possible that his vision had been clouded? That the towering, exquisite structures before him concealed a hidden layer of civilization? Were these Atlanteans more than met the eye?

The voice broke his contemplation, its deep resonance cutting through the silence like a blade. "The measure of civilization is not in the gadgets you hold dear, but in the spiritual consciousness that moves it. Cars, trains—those are nothing more than toys. Did you not see how the crown-head lifted an entire civilization from the earth's core?"

Netu blinked, as if waking from a dream. The voice continued, relentless. "What need do the Atlanteans have for your clumsy mechanical toys? They could move mountains with a single thought. A stone lifted with the mind could serve as an elevator. Why bother with machines when the mind itself was the vehicle? They mastered instant movement, collapsing distance with a mere flicker of thought. Your modern contraptions? They are lethal, cumbersome—tools of self-destruction."

Netu swallowed hard, the weight of the revelation settling in his chest. The voice was right—he could see it now. What need did they have for cars or planes when they could simply be where they wanted, no fuel or engines required? And yet... there was something crude about it all, wasn't there? Something raw in their methods, unpolished.

The voice snapped back. "Crude? You misunderstand. That 'crudeness' is the essence of life itself. Dominion over nature isn't refined, it's primal. The offshoots of your modern world are mere reflections of the true power that once flourished here. The creative minds of later civilizations only mimicked what was instinctive for the Atlanteans."

Netu fell silent, the flood of understanding swirling in his mind. The voice had made its case. They hadn't needed modernity. They had something far greater—an effortless command of nature itself.

Netu's thoughts buzzed like a flickering lightbulb, then the voice vanished again, leaving only traces of its presence—a haunting aftertaste of clarity, brief and profound. He called out for answers, for meaning, but was met with the oppressive silence of an infinite pause. Somehow, even in that void, he found a strange satisfaction.

Slowly, he stepped off the jagged rock near the river's edge, grounding himself on the familiar earth. His body felt light, almost too light, as though the weight of the knowledge he'd received had lifted his old self away. He walked gingerly into the heart of the civilization, each stride buoyed by a fountain of understanding bubbling within, feeding him like the first drops of rain on parched soil. The cold air swirled around him, rushing into his lungs, chilling, yet calming—a newness settling in his bones, as though he had shed a skin of ignorance.

His steps quickened. An eagerness surged through his limbs, an almost serpentine shedding of past inertia, reborn with strange, eternal lightness. His eyes saw differently now, as if someone had sliced through the veils of reality with a surgeon's precision, revealing the raw truths that had been hidden in plain sight. Everything appeared clearer, the distortions of history lay bare, no longer cloaked in the myths of old.

Ahead, clusters of homes stood on the left, dense and tightly packed, while on the right, a deliberate spacing emerged between the houses, breathing room in their formation. Life thrummed beneath the surface—unhurried movements, the occasional glance of acknowledgment—but the people seemed undisturbed by his presence. Under the sprawling fruit tree in front of a large house, a circle of elderly men gamed on woven mats, their eyes meeting briefly in silent competition. Only two of them noticed him, but their gazes lacked interest.

Netu passed without pause, following the unbroken path of lush green that guided him through the first clan. His feet traced the lawn until it split into a major road, branching north and south. The road gleamed, but not with the dark luster of bitumen—it was a muted red varnish, sleek and earthy. Across the road, the lawn connected again, threading through houses and paths, a seamless constellation of life. The hum of the city was louder now—chatter, clatter, the harmonious dissonance of existence—but something about the scene struck him as discordant, a creeping unease gnawing at the edges of his newfound calm.

Lost in thought, caught in the swirl of this Atlantean puzzle, a storm of confusion brewed within. His mind raced, searching for clarity, but only found the blur of overlapping realities. Instinct urged him to retreat, to seek the familiar safety of the waterfront, but then, the voice returned. It pierced through his hesitation, commanding him to stay.

"Do you think this epoch could have thrived without structure? Without governance?" the voice inquired, calm yet insistent.

Netu's brow furrowed. "No... but from what I've seen, nothing suggests it."

"How else should it be implied, if not in the very fabric you now see?"

The conversation flowed on, its rhythm soothing, almost hypnotic. The voice laid out a picture of the Atlanteans, their governance not rigid, but organic—woven into the very life they lived. Yet, for all its simplicity, it carried an undeniable weight, a reverence for order so intrinsic it needed no overt enforcement.

As he walked, his mind wrestled with the implications. The roads and houses blurred in his peripheral vision, the crowd thinning as he ventured further from the city's core. His feet moved mechanically now, leading him down a southward road, until a sharp halt broke his momentum. He scanned his surroundings, disoriented, unsure of where the path led. Behind him, the faint outline of a smaller road caught his eye—had he missed it in his earlier wanderings? He retraced his steps, mind still grappling with the voice's revelations.

"You've told me much about the Atlanteans," Netu pressed, "but what of their daily lives? Their faith, their society—how did they live?"

"They were not dead to the rhythms of life, as you might think. Their connection to the land was divine—everything they touched flourished because the earth itself responded to their needs, unbidden." The voice paused, letting the weight of its words sink in. "It was not religion in the way you understand it, but a reverence for the laws that governed the macrocosm. Their social structure was vibrant, not stifled by conservatism, as you might expect."

The voice's words painted vivid images in Netu's mind—of Atlanteans living in harmonious chaos, their society a blend of mystical wisdom and natural order. The pull of that ancient wisdom weighed heavy on him, yet it buoyed him up, light as air. He continued down the smaller road, his steps lighter, his mind sharper. But beneath the surface, something darker stirred.

Then, the voice fell silent once more, leaving him adrift in the intricate streets of Atlantis. For a moment, panic surged—had he strayed too far? But instinct took over, pulling him back toward the junction where it had all begun. The path ahead became clear, familiar now, as if the city itself was urging him to leave.

He reached the waterfront unnoticed, the stream of Atlanteans flowing past without interest. The air grew heavier as he neared the water's edge, a pull tugging at him—a yearning for home, for the familiar weight of his physical body. But before the final force drew him back, he inhaled a last breath of Atlantean air, smiling at the immense grandeur of what he had witnessed.

Netu's thoughts buzzed like a flickering light, then the voice faded again, leaving only faint echoes of its presence—a fleeting aftertaste of clarity, intense yet brief. He cried out for answers, for meaning, but was met with the oppressive stillness of an infinite pause. Strangely, even in that emptiness, he found a sense of contentment.

Slowly, he stepped off the jagged rocks at the waterfront, grounding himself on solid earth. His body felt light, almost weightless, as though the knowledge he had absorbed had lifted his former self away. He moved cautiously into the heart of the civilization once more, each step buoyed by a fountain of understanding bubbling within, nourishing him like the first drops of rain on dry ground. The crisp air swirled around him, chilling yet soothing—a newness settling in his bones, as though he had shed the skin of ignorance.

His pace quickened. An eagerness surged through his limbs, shedding the inertia of the past, reborn with a strange, ethereal lightness. His vision sharpened, as if someone had sliced through the veils of reality with a surgeon's precision, revealing raw truths that had always been there, just obscured. Everything appeared clearer now, the distortions of history exposed, no longer shrouded in myth.

Ahead, clusters of homes stood to the left, dense and tightly packed, while on the right, the houses were more spread out, allowing room to breathe. Life pulsed beneath the surface—unhurried movements, the occasional glance of acknowledgment—but the people remained unaffected by his presence. Under a sprawling fruit tree in front of a large house, a group of elderly men played games on woven mats, their eyes meeting briefly in silent competition. Only two of them noticed him, but their gazes showed no curiosity.

Netu passed without hesitation, following the unbroken path of lush greenery that led him through the first clan. His feet traced the lawn until it split into a major road, branching north and south. The road shimmered, but not with the glossy sheen of bitumen—it was a muted red varnish, smooth and earthy. Across the road, the lawn continued, weaving through homes and pathways, a seamless thread of life. The hum of the city grew louder—chatter, clatter, the harmonious dissonance of daily life—but something about it felt off, a creeping unease gnawing at the edges of his newfound calm.

Lost in thought, caught in the whirl of this Atlantean enigma, a storm of confusion brewed within. His mind raced, searching for clarity but finding only a blur of overlapping realities. Instinct urged him to retreat, to return to the safety of the waterfront, but then, the voice returned. It sliced through his hesitation, commanding him to stay.

"Do you think this epoch could have thrived without structure? Without governance?" the voice inquired, calm yet insistent.

Netu frowned. "No... but from what I've seen, nothing suggests it."

"How else would it be shown, if not in the very fabric you now perceive?"

The conversation flowed on, its rhythm soothing, almost hypnotic. The voice painted a picture of Atlantean governance—organic, woven into the life they lived, not rigid but fluid. Yet, for all its simplicity, it carried a profound weight, a respect for order so innate it required no overt enforcement.

As he walked, his mind wrestled with the implications. The roads and houses blurred in his peripheral vision, the crowd thinning as he moved further from the city's core. His feet moved automatically now, guiding him down a southern path, until a sudden stop broke his momentum. He scanned his surroundings, disoriented, unsure of where the road led. Behind him, the faint outline of a smaller road caught his eye—had he missed it earlier? He retraced his steps, his thoughts still grappling with the voice's revelations.

"You've told me much about the Atlanteans," Netu pressed, "but what of their daily lives? Their beliefs, their society—how did they live?"

"They were not detached from life's rhythms, as you might think. Their connection to the land was divine—everything they touched flourished because the earth itself responded to their needs, unbidden." The voice paused, letting its words sink in. "It wasn't religion as you understand it, but a reverence for the laws governing the macrocosm. Their social structure was vibrant, not stifled by conservatism, as you might expect."

The voice's words painted vivid images in Netu's mind—of Atlanteans living in harmonious chaos, their society a blend of mystical wisdom and natural order. The pull of that ancient wisdom weighed heavy on him, yet it buoyed him up, light as air. He continued down the smaller road, his steps lighter, his mind sharper. But beneath the surface, something darker stirred.

Then, the voice fell silent again, leaving him alone in the labyrinth of Atlantean streets. For a moment, panic flared—had he lost his way? But instinct kicked in, guiding him back toward the junction where it all began. The path ahead unraveled, familiar now, as if the city itself wanted him to leave.

He reached the waterfront unnoticed, the trickle of Atlanteans flowing past without care. The air thickened as he approached the water's edge, a longing pulling at him—a yearning for home, for the familiar weight of his physical body. But before the final pull dragged him back, he inhaled one last breath of Atlantean air, smiling at the prodigious greatness of what he had witnessed.

And then, with a violent jolt, he was gone—ripped from the ancient city and thrust back into the present, his heart still racing from the journey through time and space.

PART THREE

THE CRYPT

Silent Rage

The roar of Timipa Arabina's engine cut through the thick creek air, but it wasn't enough to drown out the sight that turned his blood cold. On the horizon, a fleet of motorboats sliced through the water, their prows adorned with the unmistakable red sun insignia of General Jacala's brigade. His pulse quickened, heart hammering in his chest. His twenty-five years felt like fifty in that instant, the weight of looming death pressing on him.

"Not today," he hissed under his breath, gripping the wheel as his gut twisted into knots. The men on the boats—hooded, wild—danced in a frenzy, a macabre prelude to what was coming. His stomach churned as if it were on a spit, roasting in the heat of his fear.

"We're in deep shit!" His voice tore above the engine's whine.

The passenger, an elegant man in a safari suit and polished Gucci shoes, whipped his head around, eyes wide. "What do you mean?" His hand, once steady on a cell phone, trembled now.

"Look." Timipa didn't need to explain further. The militant boats were closing in.

"Oh my God!" the passenger's voice cracked, his face paling as terror etched itself deep.

Timipa shot him a glance, knowing the man's well-cut suit and expensive accessories screamed trouble. Whoever he was, it was enough to catch the militants' interest—and likely their wrath.

"Pray," Timipa growled, yanking the wheel hard for a sharp U-turn. The boat lurched, throwing water into the air, drenching both men. The passenger clutched his seat, his scream barely audible over the crashing waves. The narrow creek stretched before them, lined with mangroves like silent, looming sentinels watching their desperate escape.

The roar of Jacala's boats grew louder, and Timipa's hope shrank with every second. He knew the militants weren't just after them—they were playing, closing in for the kill. The sharp staccato of gunfire cracked through the air, bullets skimming past them, sending Timipa's heart leaping into his throat. He ducked low, instinctively steering with whatever strength he had left.

"Down! Get down, or you're dead!" Timipa shouted, eyes never leaving the river ahead.

The passenger, shaking, flattened himself against the boat floor, his pristine suit now soaking in a pool of water. Timipa clenched his teeth and gunned the engine, the boat skimming the surface like a stone flung across a pond. But it wasn't enough. The militants were gaining, their twin outboard engines humming with lethal precision.

"Lord save us, Lord save us," Timipa muttered under his breath, the plea barely audible beneath the cacophony of approaching death.

Then, a voice—cold and booming—echoed across the water. "You can't run from me, boy."

Timipa's hands slipped on the wheel, his breath catching. He'd heard stories of Jacala Dadidi, a notorious militant with the moniker 'General,' but hearing the man's voice felt like staring into the jaws of a monster. Fifty meters now. Maybe less.

Timipa didn't look back. He couldn't. All that mattered was the open water ahead, and maybe, just maybe, a chance. But the river was narrowing, and as two of Jacala's boats cut around them, it became clear—escape was a fantasy.

The boats boxed him in, waves crashing violently against his hull, threatening to tip them over. And then, with a grace that defied his brutality, Jacala leapt onto Timipa's boat, landing with a solid thud that sent shivers down the young man's spine.

"Lucky for you, I'm feeling generous today," Jacala sneered, his eyes glinting like shards of glass. His red bandana whipped in the wind, matching the bloodthirsty look in his eyes. Around them, Jacala's boats circled, churning the river into a frothing mess.

Timipa barely held his composure. His lungs burned, chest tight as he fought the urge to collapse. Every fiber of his being screamed to run, to fight, but there was no way out. Jacala moved closer, his hands gripping Timipa's collar, yanking him upright like a rag doll.

"You're not worth a bullet today," Jacala growled, eyes narrowing as he studied his prey. "But you will be soon enough. Get ready to swim when I tell you."

Timipa nodded, choking on his fear. He glanced at his passenger, who now lay quivering at the bottom of the boat, his face a pale mask of terror. He knew people didn't just call Jacala a *General* for nothing. The militant had a ruthless reputation in the creeks.

"Y-yes," Timipa stammered, his voice a mere whisper.

Jacala grinned, a cruel smile that twisted his handsome features into something monstrous. He turned to the passenger, who was still trying to gather his shattered dignity. "What about you, fancy man? Think you'll make it?"

The passenger tried to speak, but his voice cracked. Jacala's boot landed square in his chest, sending him sprawling back with a gasp. "Don't test me," Jacala snarled.

The passenger, gasping in agony, said, "Yes, I can."

"That's pretty smart of you!" Jacala growled.

"But if we jump into the river, how do we get out?" queried the passenger on impulse, with his head raised slightly above the water on the floor of the boat.

"He questions my authority," bellowed Jacala. "How dare you?"

A vein of anger flashed through General Jacala's mien. He moved with deliberate ease towards the passenger and kicked him hard at the midsection. A deep groan erupted from the passenger as pain seared through his body.

"Damn it, I'm obeying your command," the passenger gasped plaintively, rubbing his midsection.

Jacala delivered another kick to the man's chest, a macabre grin playing at the corner of his lips. "This will teach you to shut your dirty mouth when General Dadidi Jacala speaks."

"But if we jump into the river, how do we get out?" the passenger asked impulsively his head slightly raised above the water pooling on the boat's floor.

"He questions my authority," bellowed Jacala. "How dare you?"

A vein of anger pulsed through General Jacala's face. He moved deliberately towards the passenger and kicked him hard on the midsection. A deep groan escaped the passenger as pain shot through his body.

"Damn it, I'm obeying your command," the passenger gasped plaintively, clutching his abdomen.

Jacala delivered anotheer brutal kick to the man's chest, a macabre grin twisitinh his lips. "This will teach you to shut your dirty mouth when General Jacala Dadidi speaks."

The passenger screamed in agony, tears welling in his eyes. Jacala's foot soldiers erupted into cruel laughter, the sound echoing across the river like a twisted symphony.

"Take over the boat, Johnbull. Move it towards the shoreline," ordered General Jacala.

Johnbull, a fierce-looking young man in his early thirties, dressed in black jeans and a T-shirt, jumped into Timipa's hydrofoil from one of the five nearby boats. With a smug smile, he adjusted his red bandana and shifted his K-47 to his left hand.

"Done, boos!" Johnbull declared, shoving Timipa to one of the seats and taking control at the stern. He signaled to his colleagues in the other boats to clear the way for Timipa's vessel to approach the shoreline. As he did., his eyes landed on a briefcase beneath the passenger's prone form.

"Hey, boss," Johnbull grinned, "lookup what we got here!

Johnbull yanked the briefcase from beneath the passenger's body. "The gods smile on us today!" He added with a sheepish grin.

"Take the money inside, but let me have my documents, please," the passenger pleaded, reaching for the briefcase.

"Looku here, man," Johnbull snarled, kicking the passenger's hand hard. "You're dead meat if you try that monkey game again."

"Please, I beg of-" the passenger began to say, but Johnbull pulled the trigger. The bullet struck the passenger's right thigh, and he shrieked in pain before plunging headfirst into the river, leaving a trail of blood in his wake.

Timipa's pulse thundered in his ears, eyes locked on the militants' jeering faces. One wrong move, and he'd be dead. He waited—tensed, every muscle ready to spring. Their laughter, loud and careless, was the opening he needed. He lunged from the ground and leaped into the river, disappearing beneath the water with a splash.

The militants' mocking laughter echoed above him as he dove deeper into the murky cold, kicking his legs furiously to distance himself. The muffled roar of gunfire vibrated through the water, but he kept low, heart pounding against his ribs. The world above sounded distant, like a dream.

Breaking the surface near the shore, he gulped in air and listened. Silence. The militants, the motorboats—gone. His boat, his livelihood—gone with them. Timipa cursed under his breath.

He spotted the passenger waist-deep in the water, shivering, his cries muted by the shock of it all. Blood ran from a wound on the man's side, mingling with the river's current. Timipa waded over, his legs pushing through water thick with hyacinths and tangled weeds. "You're still alive," he muttered, half-relieved, half-determined.

He reached the man, heaved him onto his shoulder, ignoring the sting of exhaustion in his muscles. The man's groans and labored breaths filled the silence, spurring him on. The ground beneath his feet sucked at his boots, the weight of the man pulling him down with every step.

Beneath the roots of a massive mangrove, Timipa laid the passenger down, sweat and river water mixing on his skin. Blood pulsed from the man's wound, and Timipa tore at his trousers, tying a makeshift tourniquet. The man's breathing slowed, eyes rolling back. No time.

Suddenly, movement caught his eye. Two alligators crept from beneath the mangroves, drawn by the scent of blood and weakness. Timipa froze, meeting their cold, calculating eyes. His heart hammered in his chest, but he refused to show fear. The creatures slithered away, for now.

Timipa scanned the swamp. Roots twisted like gnarled fingers above and around him. There was no way out except through—if they didn't get tangled first. The man at his feet wouldn't last much longer. He didn't have time to be scared.

"Hang on," he whispered, glancing down at the passenger. "I'll find help."

~ ~ ~

Two days after the rescue, Timipa Arabina stood beside the hospital bed, gazing at the passenger's pale face. The emergency ward's sterile scent and beeping monitors filled the air.

"You made it at last!" Timipa exclaimed, relief washing over him.

The passenger's listless body and sunken eyes hinted at the ordeal he endured. But Timipa saw hope – the worst had passed.

As recognition dawned, the passenger's gaze locked onto Timipa. "You saved my life," he slurred, struggling to sit up. The IV line and bandaged thigh hindered his movement. A pained groan escaped his lips.

Timipa rushed to his side. "Don't bother, just relax. You'll be fine."

Perede Maxwell, the passenger, brimmed with gratitude. "Thank you! I didn't even ask your name..." His voice trailed off.

"I'm Timipa Arabina."

Perede's eyes sparkled. "I'm grateful, Timipa. God used you to save me."

As they spoke, the door creaked open. A nurse entered with two visitors – a young man and a woman in her mid-thirties

"Your family's here, Honourable Perede," the nurse announced.

Perede's face lit up. "My wife, Ngozi, and son, Efe."

Ngozi rushed to Perede's side, tears streaming down her face. Efe's eyes widened, taking in his father's frail state.

Timipa stepped back, observing the reunion. Perede's words echoed in his mind: "Call me in a week... Let me see how I can repay you." The complimentary card in his pocket felt weighty – a token from a high-ranking official.

As Timipa departed, the hospital room's warmth and gratitude enveloped him, replacing the chaos of their fateful encounter.

~ ~ ~

How could anyone in his right mind do this to me?

Timipa Arabina's thoughts gnawed at him, even after leaving Perede Maxwell's bedside at the Living Proof Hospital. General Jacala had stolen his hydroplane, and with it, his peace of mind. A constant, burning frustration tightened around his chest since that day, igniting a wildfire of vengeance inside him. He tried telling himself it was one of those things beyond mortal control, but the lie only made the sting sharper. He had to strike back. But how? Jacala was no ordinary foe—he was a militant, feared and invincible. How could Timipa even dare to confront him and live to tell the tale?

The question weighed on him as he sat at the Bomadi Overside bar, nursing a bottle of Harp lager. He wiped the froth from his lips with his tongue, his mind tangled in the same endless loop of fear and anger. He belched, feeling no relief, when he saw Jude walk in, his eyes scanning the crowd.

"Jude!" Timipa waved, trying to push the brooding thoughts aside. "Over here!"

Jude, dressed in green slacks and white sneakers, swaggered over, his beady eyes still searching for something. His face lit up as he took the seat beside Timipa, shaking his hand firmly.

"I heard what Jacala did to you," Jude said, settling in. "Damn shame, man."

Timipa swallowed hard. "I swear, I wish I could strangle that bastard."

"What are you gonna do about it?" Jude's voice had a sharp edge, daring Timipa to act.

Timipa took a slow sip, eyes narrowing. "I don't know, bro. How do you fight a ghost?"

Jude's expression darkened. "Jacala isn't just your problem. He took my cousin's boat last month. Left him bleeding in the creek."

The tension in the air thickened, Jude's voice turning grim. "The guy's a damn coward. I'd kill him myself if I could."

Timipa's pulse quickened, watching the veins rise on Jude's forehead. Jude wasn't just venting; there was something brewing beneath the surface. And maybe, just maybe, it could be the key to bringing Jacala down.

"I'm telling you, Jude, I'm going to crush that bastard. It's just a matter of time."

Jude leaned closer, lowering his voice. "Hope's not lost, Timipa. Not if we know where to look."

Timipa arched an eyebrow, curious but cautious. "What are you saying?"

"You've heard the stories. Jacala's invincible, sure. But that's because he's got protection."

"His boys?"

"No, man. Not them. Something else. Something... beyond them."

Timipa straightened in his seat, feeling the chill of possibility creep up his spine. "What kind of protection?"

Jude paused as the bartender approached, placing a cold bottle of Heineken on the table. Timipa waved him away impatiently, not wanting anything to interrupt what Jude was about to reveal.

"Jacala's untouchable because of his spiritual armor. He's got protection against bullets. Hell, they say he can disappear if he wants to."

Timipa clenched his fists under the table. "So what, we just give up?"

"No. We go to someone who can take that protection away."

"Who?" Timipa's heart raced.

"Omenibo, the Egbe Priestess at Aven. She can strip Jacala of his powers."

A flicker of hope flashed in Timipa's eyes. "You really think she'd help us?"

"I'm certain. Tomorrow, we will go to Aven and see her. It's the only way."

Timipa extended his hand, shaking Jude's firmly. "Thanks, man. Jacala is going to pay for everything."

They drank in silence, each lost in their own thoughts, the low hum of music swirling around them, as the weight of what they were about to do settled in. The path to vengeance was clear. Now all they had to do was follow it.

~ ~ ~

The silvery tint of dawn barely lit the sky when Timipa and Jude sped off on a rented motorcycle at 5a.m. Mist clung to the horizon, blurring the headlights as they raced towards Aven. The road was slick with dew, forcing Jude to slow down, careful not to skid.

"Guy, look at this madness," Timipa shouted over the wind. "All because of that fool, Jacala!"

"He'll pay," Jude muttered, gripping the handlebars tighter.

By 5:30 a.m., the mist began to lift, the sun piercing through the haze. They navigated the Orho Junction, speeding up as the road cleared. At 6:10 a.m., they arrived at Priestess Omenibo's bungalow, the sun glaring like a fiery orb. The village lay silent, unsettling Timipa with its eerie calm.

Priestess Omenibo appeared at the doorway, arms spread wide. "Welcome, my children! I knew you were coming."

Timipa shot Jude a look. How did she know?

The priestess chuckled. "You thought you'd sneak in undetected?"

Timipa kept quiet, following her inside. Her eyes gleamed with a strange power, unsettling yet magnetic. The room was a shrine—chalk, cowries, and deities Timipa couldn't recognize crowded the altar.

"You seek something bigger than yourselves," she said, her voice calm yet commanding.

Timipa shifted uneasily. "Yes, Mama, we—"

"Sssshhh!" she interrupted, eyes narrowing. "I already know. You want your stolen speedboat back, don't you?"

Timipa blinked. "Yes! How—"

"I see what mortals cannot." She laughed, her voice sharp. "But beware, the lion you seek is dangerous."

"We're ready," Timipa replied, impatient.

Priestess Omenibo leaned in. "Are you? The price is steep."

Jude hesitated. "What price?"

She laid out cowries on a mirror, chanting. "Jacala, the militant, won't be easy. You need three days to prepare."

"Three days?" Timipa snapped. "By then, my boat—"

"You'll lose more than a boat if you rush in unprepared." She laughed. "Go in as empty shells, and you'll die like flies."

"Empty shells?" Jude asked, bewildered.

"Without spiritual fortification, you're nothing." Her eyes gleamed. "Now, pay the consultation fee—Five Thousand, Two Hundred Naira. We'll begin the cleansing today."

Timipa and Jude exchanged glances. "We'll pay," Jude said, handing over the money.

Within minutes, the priestess returned with chalk, gin, and kolanuts. They ate the kola, drank the gin, and received chalk marks on their foreheads.

"You're consecrated now. The real preparations start tomorrow. Be here at dawn," she said, her voice final.

~ ~ ~

Jude and Timipa arrived at Priestess Omenibo's shrine just as the light of day broke through the trees. Their hearts raced with expectation. The priestess was already waiting, her presence commanding and unnerving.

"Today's drill is different," she said, barely glancing at them as they entered. The scent of incense and something far more sinister filled the air. She gestured to two stools in the centre. "Take off your shirts."

They hesitated but complied, slipping out of their shirts and sitting on the cold wooden stools. Timipa felt a knot tighten in his stomach as he glanced at the priestess. Her movements were sharp, purposeful, and laced with a supernatural energy that hovered just beyond his understanding. He had thought he knew what to expect. He was wrong.

"Brakaemi!" The priestess' voice cut through the silence. "Bring the blades."

A young girl, dressed head-to-toe in white, floated into the room, her feet bare, her face expressionless.

She handed the priestess two razor blade sachets and a chalice filled with a thick, black liquid. Jude swallowed hard.

Priestess Omenibo ripped one sachets open, pulling out a single bade, snapping it into two. "Time to make you men," she sneered, eyes gleaming with a cruel edge. "Before now, you were nothing but babies."

She pressed the sharp edge against Timipa's chest, just above his right breast, and whispered something ancient, something dark. Then, without warning, she sliced. Timipa gritted his teeth, a sharp hiss escaping as blood trickled from the fresh cut.

The priestess laughed--a harsh, mocking sound that echoed in the small room. "A worm squirms better than you, boy!" She made six more incisions, each one faster and deeper than the last. BBlood ran in thin rivulets down Timipa's chest as she rubbed the black potion into the wounds. The burning hit him like fire, and a scream ripped from his throat before he could stop it. "Good!" She jeered. "Now you're becoming a man."

Jude watched, paralyzed, as the priestess turned to him. "Your turn," she growled.

The razor danced across Jude's chest, his body rigid, knuckles turning white as he clutched the stool, stifling his screams. The ritual was relentless.

"We move to the next stage," the priestess announced, her eyes gleaming with satisfaction. Brakaemi reappeared, this time carrying a small bowl, its contents hidden beneath a lid. Priestess Omenibo flipped it open, revealing two blood-soaked hearts.

"Cat hearts," she said matter-of-factly. "Swallow them. You'll be invincible-like a cat. No fall will break you."

Timipa's face twisted in disgust, but he knew better than to hesitate. He grabbed the heart, its slick warmth oozing between his fingers, and shoved it into his mouth. He swallowed hard, his throat burning as it slid down. Jude followed suit, gagging slightly as he forced the heart down.

:Good boys," the priestess sneered, offering them both a shot of gin to chase the taste away. "Now, for the proof."

Without warning, a young man stepped from the shadows, an AK-47 clicked, and the explosion of the shot shattered the air.

Timipa and Jude bolted from the stools, their hearts slamming against their hests as the room spun. Silence followed, eerie and complete. Then, from outside the shrine, they heard their own frantic voices, arguing.

"Come back inside," Priestess Omenibo called. Her voice was calm, almost amused.

They re-entered, eyes wide, sweat dripping down their faces. Timipa looked himself over, stunned. No bullet wound. He glanced at Jude-- nothing but the incisions from the razor. He spotted the spent bullet lying on the floor.

Laughter bubbled up in his chest. "Jacala's in serious trouble."

Jude grinned. "I thought I was dead!"

The priestess smiled, her eyes brimming with satisfaction. "That's your power. In moments of real danger, you'll vanish-just like that. Tomorrow is the final test. Prepare yourselves, Today's drill is over."

~ ~ ~

Timipa felt the sun's warmth rise over the eastern horizon, igniting something inside him. Its steady climb through thick clouds mirrored his own drive to conquer General Jacala, who had stolen everything — even his family's safety. His mind spun with plans and fear, so distracted he didn't notice when Jude stopped the motorcycle outside Priestess Omenibo's home in Aven.

"The final day of rites," Timipa muttered as he dismounted. "It should better work. I won't rest until Jacala pays."

Jude shut off the engine. "Relax, man. It's as good as done. No reason to worry."

Priestess Omenibo greeted them at the shrine's entrance, her voice calm but her expression harder than before. Timipa barely recognized her. Gone was the welcoming air of the last two days. Today, her movements spoke of purpose, a promise of something far more intense.

"Sit," she commanded, motioning to two stools near the altar. "No time for chatter today."

Her white lace wrapper shimmered in the dim light, beads hanging from her neck as she pulled a short metal wand from beneath the altar's cloth. Her eyes bore into theirs, and Timipa felt the weight of the moment. This wasn't like before.

"Fear ruled you yesterday," she said, her voice sharp. "Today, you'll become invincible by choice. You must, or you'll never defeat Jacala. He's not just a man, he's a force. No bullet can harm him, no blade can cut him. To win, you need to be more than he is. But first, I will weaken him, bring him down to your level."

Priestess Omenibo's gaze turned upward as if seeking unseen forces. She pulled a metal basin from behind the altar and poured water into it, followed by a sprinkle of native chalk and a splash of dry gin. Her incantations grew louder, filling the room like a rising storm.

"Goddess of the rivers! God of the oceans!" she cried, dipping the wand into the water. The veins on her face swelled as her power surged. "Who can stand before you? Who among mortals can withstand your wrath?"

Timipa and Jude sat frozen as her chants continued. "When a fish outgrows the river, it's time for it to die. When a man thinks himself a god, his time has ended." She paused, her eyes wild with intent. "Jacala believes he is beyond us. But I will show him he is not."

She stirred the basin again, her voice a melodic rhythm. "Come, Jacala! Come, son of the river! Appear before me!" The water in the basin darkened, swirling like storm clouds ready to unleash their fury.

The mist cleared, and there, in the water, stood General Jacala's spirit, staring up at Priestess Omenibo.

"You called, Priestess. I am here," his voice boomed from the basin, unnerving in its clarity.

A triumphant smile stretched across her face. "See?" she said, glancing at Timipa and Jude, whose shock was palpable. "Jacala answered. He's just a man after all."

The air grew thick with tension, the unseen presence of Jacala lingering like a storm ready to break.

~ ~ ~

The air in the shrine pulsed with an eerie intensity, heavy with the weight of unspoken threats. Shadows danced across the walls, but a sliver of hope cracked through the tension as Priestess Omenibo's voice sli ced the silence.

"The hour has come! Seven hours, and you must act." Her gaze was sharp, out of this world—like a goblin summoned to fulfill a fate already sealed.

"Do you have a way to Jacala's camp?" she demanded, her eyes fluttering shut in a trance of dark satisfaction.

Jude Tebedi's voice was steady but uncertain. "No, but we can rent transport when we're ready."

"That'll suffice." Her eyes snapped open. "Here, take this." She handed Timipa a slender wand, its wood warm to the touch. "This is your key to Jacala's camp. You and your hydroplane will be invisible once you point it toward his camp. You'll meet four of his sentries near his tent—use the wand to neutralize them."

Timipa's brow furrowed. "How do we do that?"

"Speak to the wand," Priestess Omenibo's impatience flared, her tone sharp. "Command them. They won't see you coming."

Jude smirked, the tension breaking for a moment. "That's quite the advantage."

Her eyes narrowed. "Forget guns. You'll need something sharper." From beneath the altar, she pulled two gleaming machetes, their edges catching the pale morning light. "These will serve you better. Lose them, and you lose the war."

The priestess rose, her movements fluid as she handed each of them a machete, the cold steel heavy in their hands. "When you stand before General Jacala, this is what you'll use. You'll find him asleep when you arrive. The rest is up to you."

She sat back down, her breath deep and deliberate. "You have the wand. You have the blades. But you'll need more than that—you'll need the courage to see this through. Are you ready?"

Timipa and Jude exchanged a glance. "We are," they answered in unison, their voices firm.

"Then go. Seven hours. That's all the time you have. I'll watch from here." She waved them off, her figure disappearing into the shadows as she slipped into the shrine's inner chamber.

~ ~ ~

The ash-colored motorboat cut across the murky creek, its whine sharp and insistent, slicing through the Angalabiri's muddy expanse. Timipa's pulse quickened when he spotted the thick smoke curling above the mangrove trees. The camp was near—just a few hundred meters. His grip tightened around Priestess Omenibo's wand, cold and firm, as the stench of rotting fish and crude oil clung to the air.

"Smooth and safe, you bastard," he muttered. "You'll pay today."

Jude, eyes gleaming with a feverish light, grunted from the stern. His heart thudded in sync with the engine's beat. "We're close," he growled.

"Take it slow." Timipa's voice was low, his eyes locked on the camp ahead.

Jude cut the engine's roar down to a gentle hum, guiding the boat through the narrowing creek. The shoreline loomed, littered with motorboats, four of them tethered and silent. Among them, one stood out—*Fortune Wheel*. "That's my boat," Timipa breathed. A flash of both rage and triumph lit his chest. "Damn, I thought I'd never see it again."

"Lucky you," Jude sneered, easing the boat to a halt by the decrepit jetty. "The hour's here."

The jetty groaned underfoot, algae-coated planks reeking of burnt fuel. Mangroves towered over them, their roots stretching ominously into the black water. Cranes perched high, their wings fluttering like silent warnings. Beneath the surface, alligators slithered into the depths, as if sensing the tension thickening in the air.

Timipa scanned the camp, his machete hanging at his side, the wand pointing forward. No movement—only the guard post, a towering wooden cubicle manned by four youths in military garb, rifles slung across their shoulders. Not soldiers, just thugs. He shot a glance at Jude. "Quiet. There," he whispered, nodding at the post.

Jude's grin faltered as he spotted the guards. "We need to get closer," Timipa said, inching forward.

Boots heavy on the path, Timipa couldn't shake the feeling they were being watched. But the guards remained oblivious, laughing among themselves. He raised the wand. "By the powers of Priestess Omenibo," he whispered, "we are invisible to their eyes."

He heard one of the guards stir. "Did you hear something?" one asked.

"Nah," the other replied, cocking his head, straining to listen. "Must've been the wind."

Timipa's pulse steadied. The wand's power held. He signaled to Jude, who crept up the derrick's side, machete in hand, taking position. Timipa followed, eyes locked on their unsuspecting targets.

Jude struck first. His machete cut through the air, severing Bonboi's neck before he could scream. Blood sprayed across the cubicle as Timipa swung his blade at Tinko, the machete landing with a sickening thud. The two remaining guards barely had time to react before the avengers' blades tore through flesh and bone, their bodies collapsing in pools of blood.

Breathing hard, Timipa wiped his blade on his trousers, the metallic taste of blood still thick in the air. He and Jude exchanged grim nods. The guard post was theirs. But their mission wasn't over.

Timipa pointed ahead. "Let's find the bastard, General Jacala."

Jude's face twisted into a savage smile. "This is his last day."

They descended the derrick silently, their eyes locked on the camp ahead. Ramshackle huts sprawled before them, but it was the two wooden buildings in the center that caught their attention.

"Jacala there," Timipa muttered, his grip tightening on the wand.

Jude followed, his breath heavy. "What's next?"

Timipa held up the wand. "Hold my elbow. Priestess Omenibo said this would be our key." He began to chant, the words tumbling from his lips as the wand vibrated in his hand, a shudder running through him. Suddenly, they vanished.

In an instant, they stood before the main building. Jacala's quarters. The door creaked open. Inside, the stench of sweat and smoke hung heavy in the air. Jacala lay sprawled on a plush sofa, his gun just inches from his hand. Oblivious.

Timipa stepped forward with the wand raised. "General Jacala," he hissed, his voice cutting through the silence. "You sleep while death knocks at your door?"

Jacala jolted awake, disoriented. "What the—?"

Jude's voice was cold. "It's over, Jacala."

The general lunged for his gun, but it slid away as if dragged by an unseen force. Panic flashed in his eyes. "Bonboi! Tinko! Where the hell are my men?" he bellowed, stumbling back.

Timipa's laughter was dark. "You'll never see them again. They're dead—just like you will be."

Jacala's eyes darted wildly, searching for a way out. But there was none. He reached for a nearby door, but Jude's machete sliced through the air, landing a brutal blow on his shoulder. Jacala staggered, blood pouring down his arm.

Timipa advanced, machete raised. "This is for my boat. For the lives destroyed."

With one swift motion, Timipa's blade struck Jacala's neck, the sound of flash tearing echoed in the room. Jacala's head hit the floor, his body collapsing in a lifeless heap, blood pooling on the Persian rug.

Timipa wiped his blade clean on Jacala's shirt, his breath steady. "Let's go. Our work is done."

Jude nodded, the distant crack of gunfire spurring them into motion. They had won, but the war was far from over.

A Tiger's Lair

STEVEN'S HEART PULSED LIKE the rush of froth in a poured beer. His eyes flicked upward, a silent thanks to the heavens, as a sleek, black Pathfinder Jeep rolled up to the curb. It wasn't just another flashy car; its gleaming surface cut through the filth of Port Harcourt's streets like a prowling predator. His grin widened as the rear window hissed down, revealing a glimpse of opportunity.

"Any mason here?" came the voice from within.

Steven's hand shot up, on the spur of the moment. "Yes, sir. Got a job for us?"

The man's voice was low and clipped. "Need two guys. Quick job. Get in."

Without hesitation, Steven tossed a look over his shoulder. "Uche, come on!" Grabbing his tools, he strode toward the open rear door, the warm sun reflecting off the Jeep's body. As Uche scrambled behind, Steven threw his tool bag inside, the plush interior a stark contrast to their daily grind. He hopped in, his skin prickling as cold air from the vents hit his face.

The stranger seated beside him barely moved, his expression unreadable beneath the shadow of his fedora. Steven's stomach churned, but he pushed it aside. This was his chance—God sent, surely.

"Uche, up front," the man ordered. His voice was steady, almost too calm. Uche obeyed without a word, his bundle of tools clutched tightly in his lap. The Jeep's windows sealed shut as it pulled away from the curb with a low rumble.

"How much for a day's work?" the man asked, his gaze hardly lifting.

Steven hesitated. "Depends on the job, sir."

"Masonry."

"Ten thousand for plastering, fifteen for something heavier."

"Twenty-five thousand each."

Steven's chest tightened, but he managed to keep his voice steady. "Thank you, sir."

Uche twisted around, brow furrowed. "Why pay more?"

"Maybe I'm feeling generous."

The man's words hung in the air, the underlying chill unnoticed by Steven, who was too caught up in the dazzle of his gold wristwatch, suede jacket, and expensive shoes. But as the Jeep slowed near a corner, a nagging doubt crept into his mind.

A man in dirty blue jeans appeared from the sidewalk, and without a word, he slid into the backseat. The doors slammed, and suddenly the mood shifted. Steven's gut clenched when the man beside him shifted, pulling a small gun from his jacket.

The cold barrel brushed Steven's side, and all the air rushed from his lungs.

A hood was shoved over his head.

"Please, we have nothing!" Steven's voice cracked, fear choking his words.

"Quiet," came the stranger's voice, firm but controlled. "No one's going to die. Just stay calm."

Steven's fingers trembled as he gripped the edge of the seat, his mind racing. The Jeep sped along, its once smooth ride now broken by bumps and sharp turns, but the route was lost to him. His prayers became frantic whispers as he tried to make sense of their destination.

The Jeep rattled to a halt. He heard the scrape of a gate, the low murmur of voices outside. The grip on his arm tightened, and he was yanked out of the vehicle.

"Easy, man! I can't see!" he protested, stumbling forward.

"Move!" barked a voice—Timo, the other man called him. Steven had no choice but to comply, his steps faltering in the darkness of his blindfold, each one taking him further from whatever fleeting hope he'd felt just minutes before.

Concrete crunched beneath Steven's feet, each step heavier than the last. He couldn't see through the thick hood over his head, but the ground shifted beneath him, betraying the uneven, interlocked blocks below. A sudden gust of air found its way through a small slit near his nose, the only mercy allowing him to breathe.

"Lift your legs, stairs ahead," Timo's voice broke through the silence, gruff and impatient.

Steven nodded stiffly, his heartbeat thundering in his ears. He stumbled at the first step, regaining balance just in time. Timo's grip remained firm, guiding him up, step by step, until they reached the top. A door creaked open. Steven felt the weight of an expansive space press in as his shoes tapped against the hard floor, each step ringing out in the emptiness.

"Here we are," a familiar voice echoed—a voice now soaked in menace. "Your job."

The hood whipped off, and Steven blinked, momentarily blinded by the sharp light overhead. As his eyes adjusted, the room came into focus—vaulted ceilings, polished armchairs, and a glass lectern. But what caught his breath were the square holes carved into the floor, yawning open near the altar. Freshly dug. His stomach lurched.

"Sand, cement. Over there." The man's voice was calm, too calm. He gestured towards two plastic drums, water sloshing inside, and a heap of sand near the exit. "You know what to do."

Uche, standing beside him, blinked away the sting of the lights, his voice thin and shaky. "What's this for?"

The answer came not in words, but in a sharp crack across Uche's face. Timo's hand had moved too fast for Steven to react. Uche reeled from the blow, clutching his cheek.

"No questions," Timo snarled. His eyes glinted, daring Uche to defy him again.

Steven's gut twisted with dread. "Let's just do it," he muttered to Uche, already moving towards the sand pile. His hands shook as he ripped into a cement bag, the fine powder spilling out like death's own offering. They worked in silence, shoveling sand and cement, their motions quick and automatic. But every glance at those holes threatened to unravel Steven's fragile composure.

"It's ready," Steven said, his voice flat, emotionless.

The man nodded, stepping forward. His eyes bored into Steven's with chilling authority. "Remember this—what you see, what you hear, stays here. Or you won't be seeing much else. Clear?"

Steven swallowed hard. "Crystal."

"And you?" The man's gaze flicked to Uche, who nodded, lips trembling.

"Bring the girls."

Timo disappeared behind a door near the altar. When he returned, he wasn't alone. A girl—small, frail—her wrists and ankles bound, shuffled forward under his grip. Tears streaked her face, her wide eyes filled with terror. Steven's heart stopped. She couldn't have been more than nine.

Timo pushed her to the edge of one of the holes. Her sobs filled the room, each one a dagger in Steven's chest. He wanted to scream, to rush forward, but his legs were cemented to the floor, as if the very mortar he had mixed held him captive.

Another girl appeared, then another—each bound, each led to the edge of their own grave. Steven's hands shook violently as he watched them, his mind spiraling. He had a daughter, not much older than these girls. His vision blurred as panic gripped him.

"Now," the man commanded, shoving the first girl into the pit. Her scream tore through the room as she hit the bottom, her small body crumpling against the dirt.

Steven's breath caught in his throat.

"Cover it," the man said, pointing the gun at his chest. "You heard me."

Steven moved mechanically, shoveling the damp mix into the head pan. The weight of it pulled at his soul as he approached the hole. The girl's pleading eyes met his, her voice an ineffectual whisper through the sobs. "Please, uncle, don't. Please."

But the man's gun pressed harder against his side, pushing him closer to the brink. The sand fell, covering her small frame. Her cries grew faint under the mounting earth. His chest tightened, suffocating with each scoop.

Timo tossed the second girl into the next hole, her leg snapping with a sickening crack as she hit the ground. Steven couldn't look anymore. He shoveled, faster, as though moving quickly enough could numb him to what he was doing. Uche, too, worked beside him, his face contorted in silent horror, tears mixing with the sweat on his brow.

"Finish it," the man growled, standing over them, the gun gleaming in the dim light.

The third girl screamed as she fell, the sound of her terror clashing against the deafening silence in Steven's mind. He was beyond fear now. Only numbness remained as he shoveled the last of the sand over her, burying her cries, her innocence, and whatever was left of his own humanity.

As the last bit of earth settled, the man holstered his gun, satisfied. "Remember," he said, voice dripping with cold certainty, "nothing leaves this place."

Steven's knees buckled. He had thought he was scraping the bottom before. Now, he was buried under it, along with the bodies of three girls whose faces he would never forget.

~ ~ ~

Steven slumped into the chair, his gaunt frame scarcely supported by the cushion, eyes dull and lifeless as he stared at the untouched meal before him. The voices of the three girls clawed at his mind, their desperate cries echoing from the depths of his memory. His jaw tightened, fighting back the surge of guilt and terror rising inside him.

"Uncle, please, save me."

The voice hit him like a lightning strike. Steven flinched, leaping from the chair. His heart pounded against his ribs as he scanned the room in frantic confusion. But the space was empty. His eyes darted toward the door, breath shallow, each beat of his heart louder than the last. He froze.

Another voice wailed through his mind, this time from the second girl, her arms bound and caked in sand and cement, pleading. "My aunt is waiting for me. Please, help me."

Steven's knees buckled. He grabbed the doorframe, his legs trembling under the weight of his fear. He squeezed his eyes shut, trying to push away the images, but they only grew sharper—the third girl now, her eyes filled with dirt, her voice like nails in his ears. "You can save me. You can still save me..."

He collapsed against the wall, his vision blurring as a wave of nausea hit him. His body trembled violently. "Leave me alone!" he yelled, voice cracking under the pressure. "Leave me alone!"

The door swung open, and Nkechi rushed in. She found him gripping the doorframe, his face pale and slick with sweat. "Steven! What's happening to you?" Her voice was filled with concern as she hurried to his side. She wrapped her arms around him, pulling him close, trying to steady him.

"I can't..." Steven's voice trembled as tears spilled down his cheeks. "God, have mercy on me."

Nkechi held him tighter, gently wiping his tears with her hands. "What are you talking about? Why are you asking for mercy? What have you done?"

Steven's breath hitched as he fell back into the chair, his head in his hands. "It's terrible... I'm cursed. Why did this happen to me?"

"Cursed? What are you talking about?" Nkechi knelt in front of him, her eyes searching his for answers. "Does this have to do with your job today? Tell me."

He nodded, his voice low, broken. "We were picked for a job—Uche and I. A wealthy man took us in his car, no questions, no details, just money and orders." He lifted his gaze, his face twisted in anguish. "We thought it was a simple gig... but when we got there... it became a nightmare."

Nkechi's eyes widened, her hands shaking. "Steven, what did you do?"

His voice cracked as he recounted the day, each detail dragging him deeper into the horror. "It wasn't just any place. It was a church. But not like any I've ever seen. We were forced... I was forced..." He paused, choking back a sob. "They made us bury them. Three little girls. Alive."

Nkechi gasped, her hands covering her mouth. She stared at him, eyes wide with shock and disbelief. "Oh, my God... Steven..."

"They're haunting me," Steven whispered. "I see them everywhere. Hear their cries. They won't leave me alone."

Nkechi reached out, touching his face with trembling hands. "You had no choice, Steven. You were under duress. God knows that. This wasn't your doing."

He shook his head violently. "No! I should've done something. I should've stopped it."

"There was nothing you could've done."

"How can God forgive me? How do I live with this?" His voice broke, raw with pain. "I don't deserve forgiveness. I killed them."

Nkechi grabbed his hands, her eyes fierce. "There's still hope. You're not beyond saving, Steven. God's mercy is greater than your guilt. Give your life to Christ, and let Him redeem you. It's not too late."

Steven stared at her, disbelief clouding his face. "You think God would forgive someone like me?"

She nodded firmly. "Yes. But it's up to you to ask for it."

Steven hesitated, his mind a whirlwind of torment and doubt. After a long silence, he wiped his eyes and knelt beside her. "I don't know if it will work... but I'm willing to try."

Nkechi's heart swelled as she smiled, her voice steady. "Let's pray together, Steven. We'll ask for God's mercy."

Cockroach-X

In the shadowy crevices of human dwellings, I've eked out a precarious existence, forever bound to the fringes. My kind has been eternally maligned, hunted, and exterminated by the very beings we cohabitate with. The whispers of "pest" and "nuisance" have become the refrain of my existence.

I've learned to thrive in the overlooked corners, exploiting the neglect and chaos that humans seem to inevitably create. But with every scurrying step, I'm reminded that my presence is a transgression, a trespass on their sanctum of cleanliness and order.

The Smart's home, my current refuge, is no exception. I've witnessed their scorn, their frantic attempts to eradicate me, to scrub away the evidence of my existence. They blame me for their own shortcomings – the crumbs, the spills, the unattended messes. I'm the scapegoat for their discomfort, the embodiment of their deepest fears: disorder, decay, and the unknown.

And so, I remain, a ghostly presence, forever on the periphery, waiting for the inevitable – the poison, the trap, the crushing heel. My existence is a fleeting, furtive thing, a momentary flicker of life in the shadow of humanity's disdain.

Mrs. Smart's shriek shattered the kitchen's serenity, her voice a razor's edge of revulsion and fury. "Cockroaches!" The word hung in the air like a challenge, as if summoning the shadows themselves to rise against me. The scent of simmering spices turned acrid, tainted by her wrath.

Her eyes blazed with a fierce loathing, every line on her face etched into a mask of contempt. "I've kept this house spotless, and now this?" Her voice trembled with restrained rage, each word a tiny earthquake. "This... abomination must be destroyed!"

With a jerky, violent motion, she snatched up a broom, its bristles quivering like a predator's claws. Her gaze scoured the kitchen, narrowing to deadly slits. "You think you can desecrate my cooking?" she hissed, her voice a venomous whisper.

The broom sliced through the air, each sweep a desperate, savage strike. The kitchen, once a haven of warmth and comfort, had become a battleground, every shadow a potential hiding place, every creak a death knell.

I seethed with indignation. "Cockroach-X"? Her words stung, reducing me to a faceless, nameless thing, an unwanted intruder. Didn't she see? I was alive, too, small but pulsing with life, my own fears, my own desires. But to her, I was just "this thing," a creature not worth a second thought.

Mrs. Smart's muttering escalated into a frenzied chant, her broom slicing through the air with deadly precision. Each sweep narrowly missed me, the whoosh of bristles sending shivers down my spine. My heart raced in tandem with her frantic rhythm, the scent of spiced meat taunting me as I fled for my life.

I darted beneath the dish, the aromatic meat enveloping me as I squeezed into the narrow gap. My tiny legs trembled, antennae twitching wildly. The broom swooshed above, unleashing a deadly waterfall of dust particles.

The dustbin loomed near the door, a sanctuary if I could reach it. My pulse pounded in my tiny body, each beat echoing the terror that gripped me. I scurried across the cool tiles, every step a gamble, every breath a risk. The broom's swoosh grew louder, closer, more menacing, but I pushed forward, desperation fueling my flight.

Would I escape, or would Mrs. Smart's relentless pursuit finally snuff out my dash for freedom? The bin's lid hung ajar, a tantalizing refuge. I plunged into the darkness, heart pounding with relief as the broom's menacing swipes receded.

Inside the bin, I nestled into the muck, my small body blending seamlessly among the detritus. The stench was overwhelming, a foul cocktail of decay and rot. But to me, this was home – a sanctuary where I could hide in plain sight. The garbage was my camouflage, the stink, my shield.

As I settled into the bin's depths, my tiny heart slowed, my efficient respiratory system adapting to the stale, foul air. I knew Mrs. Smart's disgust would keep her at bay – no way she'd dig through this mess to find me. The bin was my haven, the one place where her vanity and aversion would be her downfall.

I reveled in the irony, how humans loathed the very things they created. They blamed us for their own neglect, their own decay. Yet here I was, thriving in the filth they'd rather forget, surviving in the shadows they couldn't bear to face.

Her search dragged on, and I prayed she wouldn't think to check the bin where I was hiding. Eventually, Mrs. Smart gave up, her curses trailing off as she muttered to herself.

"I'll just have to spray some insecticide," she declared with resignation. "You may have escaped this time, but not for long."

The clatter of plates and the rush of water from the sink signaled her return to cooking. Soon, the rich aroma of onions, tomatoes, and meat frying in vegetable oil began to seep into the dustbin, masking the stench of decay inside.

I cautiously emerged, peeking over the rim of the bin. Despite the filth, a wave of relief washed over me—I had narrowly avoided capture. But the danger wasn't over. My landlady was always vigilant, and the bin was too obvious a hiding spot. I needed to find a safer refuge before she stumbled upon me again.

As the kitchen grew silent with the end of her cooking, I allowed myself a brief moment of relief. Yet the threat of the insecticide she had mentioned loomed over me, a constant reminder of my precarious situation. I knew my luck wouldn't last forever. I had to stay alert, ready to flee at any moment. The uncertainty of my fate filled me with dread, each moment a reminder that I was living on borrowed time.

~ ~ ~

Why did she have to use the insecticide?

I staggered from the kitchen dustbin, my senses overwhelmed by the acrid fumes. My antennae flailed desperately for guidance as my beady eyes stung and my trachea tightened. The air, thick with poison, clawed at my insides. Where could I possibly find refuge?

What had I done to deserve this?

Each breath felt like a struggle as I fought to escape the cloying cloud of death. Panic surged as the threat of annihilation loomed. Would this be the end? Was my survival doomed?

Blinded by the burning in my eyes, I darted into the dim master bedroom. I wove through the darkened space, dodging the oak bed and the imposing dressing mirror, and skittered toward the sofa at the far right. The harsh glare of the lights flicked on, flooding the room with a blinding brightness that exposed every corner.

The sight that met me was grim. Other cockroaches convulsed in their final throes, some struggling against the chemical's lethal grip. A few still twitched in defiance, their resistance a testament to their evolved defenses. I had to act swiftly; any delay could seal my fate.

Just then, I spotted a narrow slit beneath the sofa—my only chance. I slipped through just as the light intensified, my heart pounding, breath shallow. In the cramped, dark space, I clung to life, my senses straining to detect Mrs. Smart's movements. Her footsteps echoed as she scoured the room, the can of the insecticide in her hand a grim harbinger of death. Her curses, laden with frustration, pierced the quiet as she searched every nook.

She was determined to end my existence. Her angry rants about my intrusion into her kitchen spoke volumes. Eventually, she slammed the bedroom door and retreated. I sighed in relief, hidden once more from both the toxic spray and her relentless pursuit.

In the darkness of my hiding place, I lay still above the foam frame, my trachea burning from the residual fumes. I relied on the oxygen stored in my body and my antennae to navigate this hazardous refuge. The fear and tension were relentless, a constant reminder of how close I had come to extinction.

The truth of human vendettas against my kind was clear. They cursed us, hunted us, and used every means at their disposal to rid their lives of us. Yet, as I lay hidden, I heard the true darkness of their lives—not from us, but from their own struggles. I witnessed familial strife, financial quarrels, and deep anguish. In their quest to blame us for their woes, they overlooked their inner turmoil.

~ ~ ~

Later that night, as I ventured out in search of food, Mrs. Smart's voice reached me from the living room. Curious, I crept closer to the half-open bedroom door and saw her sprawled on the sofa, engrossed in a phone call.

Her voice carried a somber, confessional tone, tinged with an unsettling weight. I sensed the gravity of her words as she spoke to the unseen caller. My heart raced, wondering what secrets she might reveal and how they could impact my survival.

"Hello, my love," Mrs. Smart began, her voice forced and calm. "Something is really troubling my mind."

A male voice on the other end, laced with concern, asked, "What could be troubling you?"

Mrs. Smart took a deep breath, her hesitation palpable. The silence stretched before she finally spoke. "I've been trying to tell you this for days now."

The static on the line crackled, hinting at impatience. "Go on."

"I received a call from X-Land three days ago," Mrs. Smart said. "From an old friend. It's making me restless."

"Who called?"

"Leylas."

"What does he want?"

"He wants to regain custody of his child," she revealed. "But he had given up his parental rights years ago. Now he's reconsidering. Doreen thinks of Rufaza as her biological father, and you're her adoptive father."

Mr. Smart's confusion was evident. "Is Rufaza an ex?"

"No, it was just a one-night encounter," Mrs. Smart admitted. "Leylas was a choir member in our church before leaving for X-Land. He visited years later, and that's when Doreen was conceived. Rufaza came into the picture later."

"And I'm guessing Rufaza was a convenient choice as Doreen's father?"

"Yes, Leylas is Doreen's biological father."

"What will you do about this?" Mr. Smart's voice was strained.

"I don't know," Mrs. Smart answered shakily. "Leylas wants to be part of Doreen's life, but I'm unsure if it's the right move. I don't want to hurt you or Doreen."

Mr. Smart's voice tightened. "This is a lot to process. I need time."

"I understand," Mrs. Smart whispered.

As I listened, the weight of Mrs. Smart's past mistakes became clear. Her secret threatened to unravel her family's fragile structure. The tension was suffocating, and the looming revelation felt like a seismic shift.

I struggled to grasp the gravity of Mrs. Smart's confession. Her deception had long remained hidden, and now it was on the brink of shattering the illusion of her family's stability. The situation was fraught with uncertainty, and I wondered how this would all unfold.

Silence fell as they contemplated their next moves. I was stunned by the revelation, my mind reeling from the implications.

Mr. Smart's voice returned, firmer now. "Mistakes happen. I won't be judgmental. Here's the plan: I'll invite Doreen over, and we'll tell her the truth. Expect some anger, but she'll calm down eventually."

Mrs. Smart's agreement was faint. "Okay, I'll come. Be gentle with her. Leylas mentioned you're a writer and could help with his father's memoir."

"Really? That's interesting," Mr. Smart replied. "Let's see how it unfolds. This might be a blessing in disguise."

"Maybe, but his return after thirty years scares me."

"I know. Regardless of feelings, he's still Doreen's father. You mentioned he was around right after your period."

"I did. I know he's her father."

"Give him my number."

"What will you tell him?"

"Just what you've shared. We'll inform Doreen and let her choose."

Mrs. Smart's voice trembled. "He might take her away. He's promised to change her life."

"It's not his fault he wasn't there. Nor is it yours. You couldn't find him."

"True."

"None of you is at fault," Mr. Smart concluded.

The call ended. Mrs. Smart sat in silence, her distress palpable.

As a cockroach, I couldn't fully grasp their emotional turmoil, but the weight of the situation was undeniable. Human relationships, fraught with complexity and hidden pain, were a stark contrast to my simple existence. I crawled away, grateful for my uncomplicated life, unburdened by their emotional baggage.

Mrs. Smart noticed me as I emerged. Her anger flared, and she hurled a cushion at me. I darted away, narrowly escaping.

"Cockroach-X again?" she fumed. "You won't escape this time."

A Cry From the Crypt

TWO WEEKS HAD SLIPPED by since Nkem Okoro embarked on his relentless search, but the object he sought remained tantalizingly elusive. Determined, he scoured crumbling buildings, rummaged through market dumpsters, and navigated the bustling suburbs of Lagos at all hours, looking skyward for the guidance to the rune that the groove caretaker demanded.

The things we do for a taste of the fast lane, he thought, anxiety clawing at him. Just two days remained until the groove's deadline, and the dread of dire consequences loomed over him like a dark cloud.

Ugh, how do I handle this? Keep going, keep pushing! The end is in sight!

His resolve solidified, the urgency of his quest quickened. But one evening, the chilling shrieks from Shasha village nearly shattered his determination.

"*Ole! Ole!* Thief! Thief!" the angry cries echoed, chasing him as his heart raced with the specter of death. He had loitered too long around their shops and homes, a stranger in their midst.

By sheer luck, he darted down a familiar alley, anxiety gnawing at him. I hope this quest doesn't turn me into another victim.

At last, he spotted her a top a mound of refuse in a derelict building on Olarenwaju Street, her voice a disjointed symphony as she ranted at passersby in a fit of delirium. His pulse quickened.

Finally! The eagle is in the nest!

Gratitude flooded through him as he silently thanked the heavens for guiding him. Dusk's curtain needed to fall; only then could he approach her without prying eyes.

Later, he returned to find her nestled among a heap of rags, soot-streaked utensils, and filth, deep in fitful sleep. The spot was her sanctuary, a stark reminder of her broken world.

His first attempt to greet her was met with hostility. She seized a plastic doll and hurled it at him, her voice sharp and filled with fury. "You've come with evil plans to torment me! Wizard! Why don't you let me be? Go away!"

Instinctively recoiling from her piercing words, he hesitated, then forced himself to step closer.

Not now, God of the heavens! The deed must be done! Ssshh!

The surrounding darkness felt like a cocoon, emboldening him to approach.

"Not a wizard, I'm a friend!" he said, gently, holding out a tin of sardines and a loaf of bread. "You must be hungry, Tessy."

He laughter rang out, harsh and mocking, like a bird shrieking at an intruder in its nest. "He thinks I'm dumb-an illiterate! God, how is the world full of madmen? I, a graduate of English, a would-be professor! Madman, go away!"

His heart aches for her-a brilliance and beauty tarnished by life's cruel hand. As she clutched the rags that covered her, a small object tumbled from her lap into the dirt. Instinctively, he dodged, fearing another projectile aimed at him.

When the chaos subsided, he gathered his courage and returned to her side."

"Tessy, here! Take the sardine and loaf of bread. Eat, you need it," he coaxed.

"Don't call me Tessy!" She snapped, her tone sharp. "I'm Esther. Get it right, or I'll get mad! Your type pisses me off."

Her eyes flickered between the rags and the food, her hunger evident. She snatched the tin and the bread in one swift motion, cradling them as if they were precious treasures.

The stench from the refuse enveloped him-decaying matter mingling with filth, a nauseating cocktail that made his stomach churn. Desperate, he pinched his nose, but the smell lingered.

In the dim light, he noticed the layers of grime clinging to her form, hiding the beauty beneath. The torn clothes barely concealed her curves, a stark contrast to the radiant woman she might have been in another life. The dark night blurred the details, but he felt a magnetic pull to her.

"I should leave; I've overstayed my welcome," he muttered, stepping back.

"I'll come with more tomorrow, Esther," he promised, making his exit, careful no to attract attention as he blended into the shadows of the derelict building.

Even if anyone noticed him, his disguise as a scavenging street urchin--soiled hat, tattered jeans, and faded T-shirt-was convincing enough.

MY identity is safe, at least for now, until my plans come to fruition, he reassured himself

Two days later, he crept into the building again at night, and Esther's defensive demeanor began to thaw in the face of his enchanted offerings.

"Well, I have no reason to think you're mad," she said, a hint of warmth in her voice. "The things you bring me-I kind of like them."

"You do?"

"Very much!"

"More to come, Tessy. Sorry, Esther. Just be my friend, and you'll have more."

"Ehn, be your friend?"

A smirk curled her lips. "Not a bad idea!"

The first touch of his hand on her bare shoulder made her flinch, her gaze challenging him. But as his fingers danced along her skin, a warm thrill coursed through her, awakening something deep inside.

When his hand slipped to her thigh, a soft moan escaped her lips as she drew him closer. In a frenzy, he unzipped his pants.

This is it! My success story!

He had orchestrated Esther's care during pregnancy and the adoption of their child, discretly arranging everything. Now, he had the means to see his plan unfold.

Reflecting on the beginning, Nkem Okoro appeared as one of those handsome, bright-eyed men in their late twenties, prowling the streets of Lagos with dreams of grandeur. No car, no stable job, just a diploma in M<ass Communication and a background that offered little chance for advancement. Yet, the allure of the fast lane captivated him, a siren's call that seemed within reach.

He envisioned a life filled with sleek cars, lavish homes, and extravagant vacations-Caribbean Islands, Parisian nights, shopping sprees in Dubai. Money could grant access to dreams, and the world spun on its axis, governed by wealth.

Okoro's thoughts raced, fueled by the belief that success was not exclusive to the privileged. He understood the drive to succeed, the willingness to pay any price for the thrill of victory. He yearned to be among the elite, haunted by feelings of inadequacy as he watched others dance effortlessly to their aspirations.

But now, standing at the precipice of a dark choice, he wrestled with the cost. The memories of that terrified child-bound and pleading with innocent stare-tightened their grip on his conscience.

"Ah, the damn groove caretaker!" He cursed, frustration boiling within.

The shrill night calls of crickets reverberated outside the groove's walls, and an owl hooted ominously nearby. Inside, silence loomed heavy as all eyes focused on him, the weight of their expectation pressing down.

He stepped towards the altar-simple earthen pot atop a tripod, the hearth below flickering to life. Candles cast eerie shadows over the twenty-one initiates, their bare feet echoing in a haunting dance3, synchronized with the child's muffled cries.

A voice whispered in his mind: *No this isn't right. Don't do it!*

But another voice countered: *Be done with it and revel in wealth. Children will come into the world one way or another. One misguided sperm is all it takes!*

The groove's caretaker's commanding tone pierced through his thoughts. "We've wasted enough time, Nkem. Wealth requires sacrifice. You need purification now!'

The voice, though powerful, felt foreign, an unsettling reminder of his past choices. The urge to resist clashed violently with the desire to surrender to the promises of wealth and success.

He could feel both impulses wrestle for control, igniting memories of the moment he'd first stepped into this world--a neophyte turned initiate by the same voice that has led him here.

As he stood, the initiates watched him, their grotesque hoods obscuring their faces. The child's innocent gaze, filled with terror, stirred something deep within him-a primal fear, a twinge of guilt.

In that moment, he realized the choice he had to make, the path that lay before him...

THE STOLEN KNOODLE SAUCE

DETECTIVE KNUCKLEWAD HASTENED HIS strides down Abdulsallami Way, his eyes panning over the bustling crowd. Eighty-nine degrees out and hotter than a fierce oven's heat, but the walkways resonated with life. Traders, civil servants, commuters and tourists: all milling in the distance through Wuse market's gate like it represented heaven's open door, perspiring to gain entrance to its core.

The recipe is probably holed up somewhere in this madhouse, Knucklewad thought, *except that the culprit is still a mystery.*

So who did the number?

Several flights of thoughts rushed through Knucklewad right then like an inexplicable tangle of reeds. The one that lingered throughout the long night with the semblance of some significance appeared exhausted and vexed. The one that buffeted his faculties with worry still carried on relentlessly with its heady ways. The enduring voice of rationality seems to re-echo itself with banal explanations. And different other senseless echoes, lay claims to his attention.

Tossing in diverse directions like that, his fugitive mind seemed to take him nowhere. He crossed Tombia Street with the traffic's red light, pushed his way through the throng, and decided to find the grocery as fast as he could. *Maybe I'll be lucky. Or get needed hint.*

But this is still a wild chase.

Beads of sweat pooled in his close-cropped hair around his temples, rolled down his sides and back in cascades. He kept close to the first row of shops, under the shadow of the shops' awning. It helped to reduce the sun's flare on his skin, but not quite the stream of sweat.

The shop he sought glared at the corner. A huge, hot Shawarma, washed down with ice cream and chilled Chivita fruit juice, flipped on the canvas of his mind. Knucklewad reached out to that enticing vision a little. For a split moment, his thought reeled back to the force of his mission.

Then he riveted his gaze to the newspaper in his hand, and *The Guardian* headline stuck out as a sour thumb which caught his attention one more time. He stopped on his tracks, peering. Images of the hot Shawarma vanished. And the reality of something far more important flooded him with stark realization.

~ ~ ~

The ardor of the sailing sun had now waned a tint over the Abuja metropolis, but Knucklewad didn't notice this as he approached Shop 1124 at the Benin Pavilion at the Wuse market after idling around, window shopping. Even when the shop owner's assistant had to leave for an errand, he kept his calm, waiting for the right moment, remaining undetected by the man he stalked.

Same level of stealthy maneuvering went for those who noticed his endless parade, calling on him to patronize them; the boutique attendants and their pestering beckons, even when he least listened to them; the jewelers and their sonorous songs of praise of how good he'll look in the gold wristwatches, necklaces and bracelets they sold; the jesters that plied their trade in-between kiosks and shops for the largesse they'll elicit from traders and potential customers. Not even the sea of eyes ogling at him or the fear that he might blow his cover and scare the man, could wrest away from Knucklewad the control he exerted over his focus.

He took another coy look at the newspaper, trying to read the story again.

LIMP NOODLE SAUCE RECIPE STOLEN

Award winning recipe disappears from a secret food laboratory in San Francisco, USA

Police on the hunt for the unknown thief,

Still No Clues

"San Francisco Metropolitan Police Department are in shock this morning over the disappearance of the award winning Limp Noodle Sauce Recipe in a laboratory in the city. Nor can they explain why the recipe – the most forward-looking of its kind, that is believed to enhance longevity, is missing in such mysterious circumstances even with heavy security measures in place in the lab.

"As the search for the thief intensifies in San Francisco – there's an allusion to international connection, with fingers pointing at a syndicate in the most populous black nation – this, however, may be a conjecture or the machination of rumor mongers, since there are no evidences to that effect.

"A police spokesperson hinted that there's the possibility the recipe is now being sold in some hideous markets in faraway Africa and they are still without clue as to the particular location or the rationale for the brazen theft in recent history..."

Not the only strand to the story, but Knucklewad had brooded over it several times in the last few days. All led to a dead end. No matter the effort they had put into it in the Inspector General of Police's Intelligence Response Team (IRT), they were yet to find even a remote link in this part of the world to the mole that stole the recipe.

And yet the likelihood that the man he spied on at the moment might have inkling.

"Dammit," Knucklewad growled in-between breaths. "Just one lead is all I need. One slip." He felt the adrenaline surge, and his heart spiked. Inspired in some sense, he turned towards Shop 1124. He may be close to unraveling an interesting mystery today, but the facts, like the unknown persona in the hunt, still eluded him when it mattered most.

~ ~ ~

"Over there," a lady's voice goaded from behind Knucklewad, "if a good recipe is what you're looking for."

She was practically wheeling a huge trolley along the tiled floor between the rows of celeries and spices toward the eastern end of the large grocery shop, with a broad grin that seemed to say "nice you got here ahead of me."

"I was actually searching for…" spluttered Knucklewad, turning around on his heels, eyes wide and patronizing, playing the well-rehearsed ruse of a total stranger as calmly and persuasive as he ever could.

"Never a better place for groceries and recipes than this," Miss Wowzer said, yanking her trolley forward with one hand, pushing it on the tile of the shop.

As she moved away from Knucklehead, he reckoned her eyes brim with robust enthusiasm. He observed too, a number of customers steal brief glances at Miss Wowzer who looked like a happy moon with a pretty face that outshone other radiant faces, yet unaware of anything or the ogling eyes but herself and the object of her attention.

Damn too efficient for a ravising damsel, Knucklewad thought, sizing up her curves and poise, *little wonder they call her Wanda at the Wuse Police Command.* Miss Wowzer, a great burlish Igbo lady with sparkling dark brown eyes and massive bosom.

Miss Wowzer glanced backwards for a brief spell, taking in the scene.

"Gizzard on the grill," she cooed over the din of screeching trolleys and mixed voices of shoppers, giving Knucklewad some kind of cue. Then with her left forefinger she made the A-Ok sign and picked up a few apples off a shelf with her right hand.

Knucklewad whispered softly into the transmitter button on his shirt lapel. "Keep the tirade on, Wanda. No slips."

Miss Wowzer could not say with certainty why the name Wanda stuck with her at the Command, but that Knucklwad called her by it sent flushes to her cheeks. She muffled a response. "Copy that. No need to worry. We're probably on track. You just wait and see how it goes."

She halted by the last row of celeries, crossed to the other side and disappeared behind the stacks for recipes.

Knucklewad edged forward, in search of the shop's owner. He approached the male cashier at the fringe of the rows attending to customers.

"How are you doing?" he asked the cashier, setting down a few groceries in his trolley on the cashier's desk.

The cashier shrugged, tapping on the keyboard of his POS machine for the receipt of the customer who came before Knucklewad.

"Where's your boss, the owner of the shop?" he further enquired, looking around the stacks of recipes.

"Uh...sir," said the cashier, feigning a forced smile. "The office behind me."

"Alright," Knucklewad answered, flashing his flawless dentition at the young cashier as if to say "where *is the goddamn recipe?*" He warmed up instead, paid for three recipes and sashayed towards the office he was directed to.

"Is this your first time here," Mallam Azeez, the owner of the grocery asked.

"Not quite," replied Knucklewad with a drawn breath, "the second time actually." He all but needed a conversation with the man to set things going. "Just curious."

The grocer, who seemed to be a man in his early forties, raised his eyes to level with Knucklewad in surprise. "Curious?" he asked.

Knucklewad nodded, answering, "About secrets to longevity," so solemnly that even he could feel the bite of his words on the grocer.

"Death scares the shit out of me. So I'm thinking of ways to cheat death, or lengthen the experience of life," he joked, grinning. "Is there a recipe that could take care of that for me?"

The grocer hesitated. A strange impulse of thought flickered through his mind. Then he croaked his throat and said, with a calm, modulated voice, "Uh.

. . Everyone desires longevity. However, we don't have such a recipe. The Bacala recipe is a good alternative."

"The Bacala recipe?"

"Another name for healthy living," intoned the grocer, laughing. "I once thought it a scam, but after a trial, I doubt if my initial fears were justified. It may just be what you need." The grocer rose and went to the row of stacks nearest to him and fetched a green striped pamphlet. "Here," he said, handing it over to Knucklewad, "this could be helpful."

Knucklewad studied the recipe, stalling for time. "Interesting," he beamed, "not exactly what I have in mind though."

The grocer stirred curiously. "What do you have in mind then?"

Knucklewad leaned forward on the desk, thrusting the front page of The Guardian newspaper to the grocer. "This is the sorta thing I want." He placed the Bacala recipe pamphlet back on the grocer's desk.

"Bullshit," the grocer said after a moment of stunned silence, "no chance in hell. Just mere publicity stunts. No such recipe exists anywhere."

"How did you know that with certainty?" Knucklewad was not fooled by the man's glib remark. He thought he saw a flicker of recognition in the grocer's evasive gaze – a kind of shriveling from the truth.

"Bullshit," the grocer shot back. "If a recipe for longevity exists, I'll be one rich man smiling at the bank daily. Forget it sir. A figment of the mind."

Knucklewad shifted his frail physique as if to give up on the grocer's fluid argument, but instead fixated his gaze on the grocer. "Would someone like you be willing to risk it all to acquire such a recipe if it exists?" It was a banal attack, a gamble, Knucklewad knew, but prayed on the inside for the grocer to make a slip in tongue or give his guard away.

The grocer looked at Knucklewad with a stern visage. "What are you? A detective? I just told you, I've no idea a recipe like that exists."

"Don't take offense sir," Knucklewad soft-soaped. "I'm just a curious customer. "Any other grocery I should check in relation to this?"

"If you would excuse me, as you can see, I'm a very busy man," stormed the grocer. "Good day sir." With that he focused on the cash ledger on his desk, dismissing Knucklewad with a frown.

Knucklewad did not miss the grocer's tell-tale tantrum. Quite unlike a serious-minded businessman to get irritated so easily over trifles. Something didn't sit well with his jumpy attitude, Knucklewad thought as walked out of the grocer's office back to the main hall of the grocery.

"Wanda, any sitrep?" Knucklewad asked, almost in a whisper over the transmitter button on his lapel. A brief hum at the other end and Miss Wowzer's voice filtered through the receiver in his ears.

"Yes, Curly," Miss Wowzer replied with a tinge of elation. "Got a useful lead. Details on our way out."

"Spill, Wanda. Met a dead end here, but I'll be damned if I didn't feel a sense of unease with our man," he said in a hushed tone as he negotiated the grocery's exit door. "Done shopping here for today. Will be back soon though."

"Nyanya market is our next berth. A name popped up. A group of die-hard hustlers in recipes have a base there."

"Good lead."

"Thank you, boss."

"The pleasure is mine," Knucklewad said. "Rendevouz at Nyanya market then."

"Copy, Curly," Miss Wowzer's excited voice boomed in his ears.

This is becoming interesting! he mused. A gush of fresh air teased his face as he meandered his way through the multitude of shoppers leaving Wuse market's main gate. There just might be a saving grace in Nyanya market after all.

- Culled from **_WHOLE WIDE WORLD –_** **_An Episodic Crime Thriller_** published by SweetyCat Press, USA.

www.ingramcontent.com/pod-product-compliance
Lightning Source LLC
Chambersburg PA
CBHW060657190726
48289CB00002B/446